DISBELIEF

Smirnov Bratva Book 2

T.L. Smith

T.L. SMITH

Disbelief

Book 2

T.L Smith

Copyright 2016 TL Smith
All Rights Reserved

Cover – Romantic Book Affairs

Formatting - Angels-Indie-formatting

Editing by Swish Design & Editing

Proofread – KMS Editing

Cover image – by Wander Aguiar

Dictionary

Pakhan – Mob Boss

Bratva – Russian Mafia

DISBELIEF

Noun – Inability or refusal to accept if something is true or real.

BLURB

What if I was to tell you, you're all evil?

In some shape or form, you are.

What If I was to tell you, I was the worst kind of evil?

Would you believe me?

I did not believe that there wasn't anyone who didn't contain evil.

I was proved wrong, and it stumped me.

I became obsessed with her, someone of pure goodness.

And couldn't get enough.

I needed to see her insides because that's what I do. Tearing people apart, I have to prove my point. I wanted to split her apart, to find any trace of bad.

It was wrong of me to think like that.

Though if death is all you know, is it so wrong?

My name is Death. Her name is Pollie.

And I want to see her insides.

Just to understand if she is as pure as she makes out to be.

PROLOGUE

My first hooker, I was sixteen. I fucked her three times, and on the fourth time, she wanted to introduce me to something new, something different.

She was my first fuck. My brother paid for her, sent her to my room, and she fucked me. I'm not going to bullshit you into thinking I'm a sex god, I was far from it. My family didn't talk about sex, and I wasn't around anyone else to discuss it. I went to school, never spoke to anyone, then came home to watch my brother cremate the dead. That was my life. I didn't even notice girls. He seemed to realize this fact, and so he sent her to me—paid her to fuck me.

It lasted seconds. She told me I was her best— she bullshitted me. So I hired her for a second time and lasted longer that time. I was proud, and I was getting the hang of it. Then the third time, I fucked her for at least fifteen minutes straight, slamming into her again and again.

She sat at the end of my bed that night. We didn't speak, we never spoke. Well, no, let me rephrase that, I never did.

This time, she wished to speak. "I want to try something new," she said as she lit a cigarette and placed it between her lips.

I watched her mouth as she pulled it away then blew it out causing the smoke to circle and her mouth to form an O. I'd almost forgotten what she had said until she started again.

"You learn fast, and I know you're clean." She looked around my pitch black room. "Well, cleaner than your brother." She laughed and then walked to the window, flicked the cigarette outside and stepped back to me. Her lips touched the back of my ear. "We're going to try blood play."

I shivered, I was excited. The sound of those words intrigued me—too much.

I wanted to ask my brother later that night if he knew what it was. I didn't understand it, any of it. But the idea alone, I was more than interested in. She came to me, stripped, and stood in front of me completely naked. Then she pulled a small bag from her purse. She laid it down and opened it up like it was some kind of toolkit. And that was exactly what it was. I didn't know at that moment, but she was about to fuck me over. Make me more twisted than I already was. She would change my idea of sex and passion at the age of sixteen. She did, she fucked me completely.

Then from that day on, I never fucked just for the thrill of getting my cock wet. I was in it for the excitement, the high that came along with it. Let's face it, hookers would let you do anything as long as you paid them enough, and I always had plenty of money. My family was loaded in it.

Not once in my life have I fucked someone that I haven't paid.

Not once have I fucked someone that was just for the pleasure of them.

It was for all the wrong reasons and the vile thrills I'd get from it.

I wasn't ordinary, my life was definitely not conventional.

I was fucked, and I relished in it. Loved it. I was as twisted as a pretzel, and burnt as a marshmallow cooked over a bonfire. And anyone that got too close would end up the same way.

CHAPTER 1

Death

It was never that I didn't like girls—hell yes I did. I liked their bodies, but not their minds. Except Pollie's. I became possessive and didn't want to let her go. And I knew from that moment that I was fucked. So I did the only thing I knew, I wanted to kill her. Well, a part of me wanted to kill her. I didn't want to be stuck under some spell. I didn't want to become one of those men.

I was *not* one of them.

I didn't have a mother figure or even a woman that featured in my life. I had nothing but violence and death.

I was given that name when I was sixteen. From the moment I knew that I enjoyed taking a life and that I loved playing with that life once it was extinguished. I wanted to do bad things, I wanted to slice and dice someone, and I didn't want an audience. So I isolated myself, only coming out when I had to.

Pulling myself from my thoughts, I feel the smile tug my lips, and the shock written over Elina and Kazier's face. I did warn him, I know I did. If I had those types of feelings for a woman, I would slit her throat, because that's what I assumed love would be—my own death.

I don't want death—I haven't finished handing out my own deaths. I relish in death and delivering it gives me a sense of achievement and wonder. I admire death in all its forms, whether given or received.

The knife is digging deeper and I can feel Pollie begin to shake underneath it. I'm about to cut her, I can feel my hand wanting, no needing, to go deeper into her white, tender skin. I desire, by my hand, to watch her life extinguish and the blood drip from her wound.

Why did she have to be it?

Why did I have to choose her?

The moment I saw her I knew. I knew that I wanted her, it was instant.

She's opposite of everything I am.

Not one thing between us matches, not one. Her sweet voice, to my rough. Her kind nature to my tough exterior.

She can't see me, and for that I am thankful. She shouldn't see someone like me, someone so utterly damaged. The moment, if she could see me, she'd run the other way. Instead of coming to me.

Her hands start to tremble, the same small hands I like to have in my own. Her hands are always warm, always comforting. Maybe that's the reason I want her all the time? Because she's the opposite of everything I know or have encountered. There's not a bad bone in her body.

A part of me wants to lift the knife, the other is glad she'll see me for what I am. The moment she started playing her violin, I felt it, like it slammed into my chest all at once.

Perfection.

And someone with so much perfection shouldn't be allowed on this earth. This earth is full of so much evil, I thrive in it. It keeps me placid, peaceful. The good, well I haven't encountered much if any of it.

Maybe that's why I want to kill her. So I can see what her insides look like, to check if they're as clean as she is on the outside.

I can hear voices yelling, but none of it registers. None of it seems real. The only real thing in this life is the knife I'm holding to her neck.

I want them to stop screaming at me.

No, I want someone to stop *me.* I know I do.

But that won't prevent me from what I'm about to do. Not unless I'm dead.

This is the first life I can feel struggling in my hands. One I know I shouldn't take, but I still very much want to.

I can hear my father in my head, taunting me.

"*Do it! You won't be a man 'til you've done it. Are you a girl? Are you?"* he screamed the last part.

After my first kill—the blood lust didn't stop it only got worse. The more and more he put in front of me the more I craved it and wanted it more and more.

I like what I do, but I love the after part. The watching of someone who was living only a few hours before come apart on my table. Like they don't know, but their eyes tell me differently. Their eyes are always open, staring out into space. I always feel that their stare is penetrating me.

Maybe it is. Maybe they know, somehow, somewhere, that I'm about to lose myself as I tear them limb from limb.

Her violin echoes when it drops to the floor, the sweet melody she was playing earlier halted. Now only silence fills my head. Nothing but damn silence. I can't stand it and must have some kind of noise around me. I prefer music, music that will make my ears bleed and my heart scream.

A shot rings out, it whizzes through the air then hits me straight in the chest.

A small smile tugs at my lips, probably the first one in a long time.

I need that, I need to be stopped.

A scream, and I know that voice—it's Pollie.

Oh, Pollie, why must you be you?

My head hits the floor hard, my body dropping backward. I watch her stand, her long hair falls around her shoulders, and that's the last thing I see before the blackness encases me.

CHAPTER 2

Pollie

Their hands touch me, grabbing at my neck. My hands push them away, and I manage to sit up on the floor where I landed. Elina's trying to see if I'm injured, her hand runs along my neck, wiping away the blood I can feel as it oozes from the wound.

She warned me, maybe I should have listened. She said her people were bad. That they were not to be trusted. I didn't feel that way with Death. He was quiet and reserved. Every time I was in his presence, he would grab my hand. His large, strong hands would encase mine, wrapping them up like I was a child. I kind of liked it, not because I couldn't see, but because he felt the need to hold them every time we were together. Even when we were sitting, he had to hold them.

The last man I was with used me. He took my disability and played me like I play the strings of my violin. I didn't see it coming, he was always so caring and nice. It was all an act. I remember the day I found out that he'd taken all my savings. Every last cent that my parents had left to me when they died. I'd mistakenly told him about my money, and he's used that information to steal from me.

It is hard to think that someone who shared the same bed as you—the same person who would touch your body and whisper sweet nothings in your ear—would take advantage of you. But I didn't let it consume me, or let it anger me. I never wanted to be someone that holds anger so that you lose yourself. If you do that you become a person you're not familiar with, someone who's not you.

So I shook it off and worked harder. Blocked him from my mind. Stopped all access of his thoughts in my mind. He could no longer enter the house I owned, and he could no longer have the car I'd bought him. Instead, I sold it and replenished a small amount of the funds he'd stolen. To say he wasn't happy was an understatement. He would come to my house and bang on the door all night, hoping I'd let him back in.

Why would I do that? So he could use me again? I may be a nice person, but I have my limits and I'm not stupid.

"You're bleeding," Elina says, placing a cloth to my neck.

Touching where the blood is coming from, I realize the cut isn't deep. I could feel his hesitation when he held the knife to my neck. I could feel his heavy panting as he breathed down over me.

I want to hate this man, and I don't want anything more to do with him. He scares me, there's no doubt about that, though he excites me as well. I've never met a person more closed off than Death, he doesn't even tell people his given name. Hell, you're lucky to even get a few words uttered at you.

"I'm fine," I say reaching for Elina, my hand making contact with her shoulder. I feel her slump.

"I want to keep you around. You're the only true friend I've ever had. But I don't think I can…" I can hear the crack in her voice, the disappointment. I listen as legs run past me, and I strain to hear as Kazier starts swearing at Death, the cursing becoming louder and louder.

I can hear the thump to Death's chest as Kazier tries to revive him. I crawl my way over following the noise, and as soon as my hand makes contact I know it's Death. His large hand lays lifelessly on the cold tiled floor. I can't hear him breathing. My hands start to skirt upward, wanting to touch him—to make sure he's still alive. I don't want him dead. It'd be the last thing I'd ever want from him.

"Death…" My voice is harsh, my mouth and eyes are now dry compared to the wetness that was covering them only moments before. I'm now worried, my hands are shaking, my voice is hostile. I start to shake him and hear Kazier swearing at him. Then I listen to the front door being pushed open, footsteps echo in the hall then come to stop near me. I feel a hand touch my shoulder.

"Miss, I'm going to pick you up."

I don't answer in return, I can hardly speak now.

Is he dead?

Did *I* do this to him without even knowing?

I know it's not my fault, and that I didn't put the knife in his hand. But what I have come to understand is that he's not like most people—he's very different. Unlike anyone I've ever met.

His mind works opposite to most. Where we think safety, he thinks destruction. Where we think good, he thinks of only evil. I don't know why. I don't understand why. A part of me really wants to understand, but then a part of me on the inside screams to run. Run as fast as I can and as far as I can away from him, but I'm not listening to that last part right now.

Right now, hands wrap around my waist, and I'm lifted into the air as if I weigh nothing. It reminds me of the gunfire at the club when I was at with Elina. How Death carried me out like I weighed not a thing. The hands hold me place me on a table, then those same hands start to wrap my neck, but I don't know why.

I can't feel the blood that was dripping down my neck anymore. So I reach down and touch my shirt and feel the stickiness of the blood that's semi-dried—it's more than I remember.

"It looks like you don't need stitches. Did you hit your head at all, Miss?" the stranger asks me. I listen as I hear the "oomph" of men lifting something heavy. Then heavy footsteps walk altogether.

They must be carrying him.

"Is he okay?" That doesn't sound like my voice. I don't even recognize that voice.

"He isn't responding. He is breathing now, though." Kazier's strong voice booms close to my ear. "I need to go with him." This time his voice isn't directed at me.

I hear Elina's response, and try to get down from the table.

A hand stops me—Elina's. "Where do you think you're going?"

"I want to make sure he's okay."

"No. You don't need to be around him anymore. He can't be trusted."

I shake my head slowly from left to right, even though I know she's right. He can't be trusted. Doesn't mean I want him to die, though. I need to make sure he's going to be all right.

"I'm going to drive you home." Elina hands me my stick as I climb down, my hands still shaking. "Will you be okay? Do you want me to stay with you?"

"No, I think I just need some sleep." She guides me to her car, not speaking as we slide in. The silence is not something I'm wanting, I don't crave the quiet. Never have. I always need something, anything, and keep it loud. The silence scares me, kind of like the dark scares most people. Still, nothing is said on the drive. The calm is crushing me.

"You sure you don't want me to stay?"

I reach for the door handle, pulling it open to get out. I stop but don't turn to face her. She might see some cracks if I did. "You just got engaged, spend it with Kazier. I'll be fine."

Her hand touches my shoulder, and she squeezes softly. "I'm sorry, Pollie. So sorry."

"It's fine. It wasn't your fault."

"I should've kept you away. I should have insisted."

"You can't control me, I wouldn't have listened no matter what you said."

"I'm going to call Maso. I just want him to come and check on you. Okay?"

I start to shake my head. "You'll just make things worse. You already have issues with your family."

"This may turn into a war, just because of the person I love. Yes, true, but he's my brother, and he loves me. So he will do it."

I knew there'd be issues. Major issues. She's with her family's sworn enemy and a dangerous one at that. No good will come out from it. She should be worried about herself, not me.

"I'll be fine," I say effectively ending the conversation as I leave the car, shutting the door and walking to my apartment building.

CHAPTER 3

Death

I lie here awake, but my eyes are closed. There's blackness all around me, darkness all around me—gloom, shadows, death. Then there's my family, who's considered dark, scary, the most likely to kill. I knew this from an early age—a very early age. At the age of ten, I saw my first body.

Yes, at the age of ten—you did hear that right.

That was the age I touched my first body. My brother worked in the family crematorium much to my father's disappointment. He's always been close to Kazier's family. My father did all the dirty work for Kazier's father, all the things that most didn't want to do. He was their hitman. My brother didn't like that part, so he turned to death. Destroying the bodies, defacing them so they could never be recognized.

The day my father was shot to death, I was

twelve. A role was expected of us—my brother and I—we were to take over from my father, to become the next hitmen of the family. We didn't want it. Neither of us desired that assignment. Sebastian took the role because I was too young. He's five years older than Kazier and I. So he was expected to lead our generation, the next generation.

I became intrigued with what he'd do at night after his kills. How he would creep to the basement of our family home, dragging a body wrapped in black plastic.

He'd see me standing at the top of the stairs every night waiting and watching for him to enter, then he'd wink at me as he hauled that body inside. I would wait until I heard the thump, thump, thump, down the stairs. Then I'd creep down them just a few steps and sit watching, as he either cremated or dismembered the body.

"It intrigues you," he said one night. I never spoke much, so all I gave him was a nod. He scratched his chin with his hand that was still gloved, then he looked up at me. "It's very lonely." He stopped when he said that last part, then smirked up at me. "It would suit you," he said thinking about it, then waved his hand for me to come down and watch.

Every night I'd follow him down and observe what he was doing, eventually taking over when I was sixteen. It was tiring to him—all the death and destruction and then came the after part—I could see it on his face. I don't think it was so much the death that tired him, but who and how often he was doing it. He wasn't a fan of Kazier's father, he actually despised the man. So when I turned eighteen years old, I knew everything was about to change. I knew it the moment he came home one night without a body and just a gun tucked into his pants.

I had started inking my skin, so far I'd only had half of my body covered. You couldn't see a clean piece of skin on my left side.

"I'm leaving." His voice sounded like it penetrated through the walls at that time. Like it was an echo, and it wasn't real. Both my parents dead, the only person I had left was Sebastian. Even if he didn't show me affection, even if we hardly talked, he was it. "I'm going to Russia. Pakhan can't say no. Not to this. I can't stay in the hopes that one day I won't have to do the parts I don't want to do. I prefer the aftermath, just like you. Pakhan won't give me that, he wants me as his hired hand. So I am going to work for Alexander. He's struck a deal with Pakhan, that when Kazier comes of age, he will

marry his daughter. Pakhan can't say no to Alexander." My head dropped. Sebastian didn't try to soothe my feelings, he didn't know how to. Hell, I didn't even know how to. All either of us knew was death.

I stayed clear of Kazier's father for as long as I could after that night and hardly left my house. Knowing he'd requested I take over my brother's work, I tried to avoid him. It was something, just like my brother, that I never wanted to do.

Then just before I turned nineteen, Kazier and his father walked into my house. They asked me what I wanted to do, and I informed them I wanted death, nothing more.

So death is what I got, and death is how I live.

****

The years ended up blurring together, night after night I'd get a call to clean up. I now had a team that helped me carry out my tasks. They cleaned the mess at the scene, while I destroyed the bodies. It's been like this for years. I ended up becoming more and more reclusive, talking to hardly anyone. Scarcely uttering a word unless it was needed.

My brother's calls became less and less the

older I got. He would phone to see how I was doing, that was the extent of the calls. I'd even spoken to Freya's father, he had offered me some work. He didn't seem anything like Kazier's father. He appeared more respected, and he gave respect. He spoke of my brother as if he was a godsend, and he wanted me. In the end, I refused. I'd become accustomed to my work, I loved my work. It didn't involve speaking to people unless I had to. My work was just me and the dead body on the table.

I stopped cremating bodies when I was twenty when I moved from my family mansion and left it vacant. I didn't want to live in that house anymore. It was too big and contained too many reminders. So I bought a small apartment under the condition it had a basement. I didn't want to travel back to that house every night to cremate, so I improvised. I dabbled in learning new techniques. I even bought a pet shark, but that didn't work out as well as I had planned. My apartment was far too small. Therefore the tank was too small. So I killed it, watched as it suffocated and died. Death, what a fascinating thing it is.

Then when I was in the hardware store one day I discovered acid. And what a beauty that turned out to be. I loved it, more than I adored fire.

Music would be on—loud—my body covered. I would get lost in the sizzle, the breakdown. And before long it became me. The death.

I wasn't born with that name. Death. I actually picked the name up along the way. Kazier joked one day and called me Death. I nodded my head, and he was surprised. And now it's the only name everyone knows me by. Only Sebastian calls me by my given name.

Sebastian found out about me leaving the house, and about not using the cremator. He was intrigued to see what I do now, how I get rid of the bodies. I told him what I was doing, and he rang back the next night to tell me he couldn't handle it. He couldn't stand the smell. I didn't understand, it had never affected me. Then I could hear his emotions seep through the phone line, he was worried about me.

Worried about how dark I'd become—was there anything left inside me. He said the killing part he couldn't handle. He wouldn't hesitate to kill, he just didn't want to take part in doing that anymore. That was why he chose death because it was easier. It is. I don't disagree, at all. The person can't speak back, they don't whinge and whine for their life. They just lie there, their soul already left. So it's just a vessel, one I relish in destroying.

He wanted me to come to him. I refused. I didn't want to go anywhere. He pled with me to ask for a change of job. I also refused. So when he found out I was now under Kazier, he was pleased. He knew I'd isolated myself at home, he knew I hardly spoke to anyone but him. His voice sounded like optimism. I didn't tell him I was made to do this job and that I had no choice. I just didn't want to. You don't say no, you never say no to your Pakhan. If you did, there was only one way to go. And it wasn't in a body bag, it was in multiple body bags.

Working with Kazier hasn't been that bad. I've always held respect for him. He's nothing like his father who will walk over anybody to get where he needs to be. No, Kazier is ruthless, don't get me wrong. His fascination with blood is what mine is with death. He loves the kill as much as I love the aftermath. Though, he's creating drama, very unwanted drama for the sake of love.

Love, I still don't understand it.

He fell for the wrong woman, a woman who's part of a family that's our sworn enemy. Has been for as long as I remember, and more than likely will continue to be so until after I'm dead. It doesn't matter that she hates her family, it doesn't matter that they refuse to not be together. I will fight for him. I will kill for him. His choice in love won't stop me from protecting him. My loyalty doesn't lie with that, it lies with him solely as a person.

Kazier was the reason I've kept to my job for as long as I have. He's the reason I have a team, the reason I have money. He gets me what I want, what I need. He pushed his father, I know this, he's told me so. He warned me one day that he would call on me, I just didn't expect it to be so permanent. The only plus side is, he still lets me do what I want.

A part of me wants to kill Elina, just for the simple reason of bringing Pollie into my life. I don't need these emotions, or whatever they are that course through me every time that woman is near. I don't even understand it, let alone want them.

I think she did understand it. Pollie was always calm around me, which made me intrigued by her. Was it because she couldn't see me? She couldn't see what a monster I was, inside as well as out. I have ink on my face, tear drops from a child I had to get rid of. It wasn't something I wanted to do, and as soon as I carried out my task, the tear drops were etched onto my face to signify and never forget them. To cry for someone that could cry no more, and to cry for me because I've not shed a single tear for as long as I can remember.

The child was caught up in something that he shouldn't have been involved with. His mother was a drug user who owed money to multiple dealers. When our team went there to procure the cash, gunfire was shot into her home and a child was inside.

Evil, everyone is evil.

A mother is evil, choosing drugs over the health and well-being of her child.

Women are evil, using what's between their legs to get what they want.

Men are evil for using their power and fortitude to get exactly as they pleased.

The world is full of it—except Pollie.

I don't understand her.

I'm afraid I never will.

I'm afraid I will kill her before I figure it all out.

****

I can feel Kazier's hands on me, closing the wound. My mind drifts in and out. I wake to his face hovering over me, then close my eyes and watch my past play in my mind. When I wake again,

I'm in my bed. My shoulder's bandaged, the past has stopped visiting. Now it's just dreams, dreams of her.

Kazier walks in as I sit up, the strain from my shoulder pulling like a bitch from where his woman shot me. He shakes his head as he stands at the door, looking to my wound then back to me.

"You're lucky she's a good shot, she could have killed you. She should have killed you for being that fucking stupid." He turns to leave, then looks back at me. "Try to stay away from her." He closes the door quietly as he leaves.

It wasn't a threat, just advice. A caution I will try to heed.

CHAPTER 4

Pollie

Elina tells me he survived. That he's going to be fine with some time. She's said I'm not to go to him. That I shouldn't make contact with him again. He is dark, dangerous. I asked her to describe his appearance to me as I want to know how he looks on the outside. I've peeked into the inside, but he's very closed off, and I want to know more. Curiosity is getting the better of me.

It's been almost a month since that night, and a month since Elina and I have seen each other. She calls, but doesn't offer to meet with me. I don't want this incident to affect our friendship, she's my closest friend. I don't have many, mostly only those who I work with.

I currently play in musicals, very highly paid musicals. I've worked my way up. Practice and talent have earned me the concertmaster position of the orchestra's first violin section. I've never turned down any offer, no matter where it was including traveling all over the world, and I've made some very high-profile friends. But I always come back home, because I couldn't imagine living anywhere else. This is where I still feel my family, and sometimes I need that reminder that I was once unconditionally loved.

"How's the engagement coming along?" I ask Elina. Noticing my hands are sore—I've been practicing too long—I rub them together trying to ease the pain.

"He wants a party." I hear the whine in her voice.

"You don't?" I ask confused.

She laughs through the phone. "No. That's like bringing the war to my door. I don't want that. Someone will get shot, possibly even killed. Can you imagine? Congrats… then boom," she says the last part loudly with a small nervous giggle.

She told me a while ago that the night she drove me home she was sending her brother over. I won, and he didn't come, so I wonder if he'll even be invited. If any of her family will, in fact, be invited.

"Do you celebrate engagements?" I remember vaguely her saying that Kazier's family didn't.

"My family does, he knows this. His family... no. Not unless it's for a publicity event."

"I want to come."

"Pollie..." she stops then whispers into the phone, "...Death is coming. He's a part of Kazier's family."

"I know, I wouldn't ask for him to not to come. I'm fine with seeing him, Elina."

I actually think I am okay with it. Well, I'm hoping I am anyway.

He wouldn't do it again. Not with everybody around, would he?

"I don't know."

"Is your brother going?"

"He is. He isn't by any means on friendly terms with Kazier and his people, but he respects it."

"Good. Get him to come get me. I can go with him." I don't want to, but I think that's the only way she'll say yes. No matter how her relationship is with him, she loves him, and he protects her.

"Okay, it's tomorrow night, I'll call him now.

Just promise me if you feel uncomfortable, you'll tell me instantly."

I tell her, "Okay," and wonder if it's the right thing to do. To be near him again.

****

My dress clings to my body, I can feel how it wraps around and grips to all the parts I usually keep well hidden. My usual attire is plain—simple jeans, shirt, and a scarf. Tonight, I wanted to dress up, knowing that everyone will be clothed smartly. I don't want to be looked down on anymore. It's not all about my disability, I hear it in their voices when people compliment me that they are not telling the truth. Like, I can't read how their voice hitches up a notch while telling their lies.

A knock comes on my door, and I know it's Maso. My last encounter with him didn't go well, I could sense his stare. It wasn't a curious stare, it was more a come-hither feeling. I know that feeling anywhere, I've felt it for most of my life. Men love to watch, love to ogle. My senses are hyper aware, and they don't realize that their stares feel just like a grope or a fondle. I can feel it inside me, inside my core, but they're oblivious to my awareness.

"Pollie," he greets when I open the door. His hand comes to rest on my hip, then he draws me in and kisses my cheek. I hear his minute intake of breath as he breathes me in. It makes me uncomfortable, and I pull away.

"Thanks for this, Maso," I say, reaching around and grabbing my bag and my cane. Maso hooks his arm through mine as we walk out of the building, and he opens the door of his car. I sit quickly and listen as he climbs in, starts the ignition and pulls out into the traffic. "Are you nervous?" I ask him out of curiosity. He is, after all, going to a gathering that's contradictory to his beliefs—these are supposedly his sworn adversaries. People have died for less from what Elina tells me.

"No. Though I would be if my father knew I was going."

"He doesn't know?"

"No. If he knew, you can guarantee bullets would be fired. This won't be easy for them, our families despise each other. We've killed each other for less. This, my father's daughter marrying the enemy, I can guarantee blood will be spilled. I'm just here to make sure it's not hers."

His honesty takes me aback, I didn't expect that kind of answer or the devotion in his voice. He clearly loves his father, though his protection of his sister out rules that all.

"You don't think Kazier can protect her?"

He laughs dryly. "Yes, without a doubt. If anything, he'd kill everyone to protect her... even his own family. That's what I'm worried about. If that happened, it would be a bigger clash than what's already started."

The car comes to a stop and I open the door, but before I have a chance to get out, his hand is on my arm, guiding me.

"Your tits look great," he tells me.

I shake my head, knowing full well he has a massive smirk on his face. "For a second there I thought you were a decent human being. Then you had to go and say that."

"Just stating the facts!" I feel him shrug as he guides me up the stairs.

Hearing music and laughter when we enter, Maso keeps a firm grip on me as we make our way through the crowd of people. He halts, and I know he's stopped in front of Elina. Her aroma is truly unique. She layers her scents, and I can smell the jasmine emanating from the shampoo she uses combined with the body perfume she's wearing. With my heightened senses it's a beautiful combination, I can always tell when she's around.

"I'm glad to have you here, Pollie," Kazier expresses. I smile, and Elina leans in and kisses my cheek then takes my hand from Maso guiding me away.

We walk a few steps before she speaks, "He didn't hit on you, did he?"

I laugh and shake my head. "Nope. He just complimented my breasts."

She stops walking. "He did not! Do you want me to smack some sense into him?"

I shake my head and pull her forward to continue walking. "I can't leave him alone too long, I don't fully trust everyone here," she says referring to Maso.

"He loves you deeply, you know. He only wants to protect you."

"I know… trust me, I know. He just hasn't realized I can do that myself." She stops to talk to a few people, introducing me to some. I shake hands and smile, giving nothing else. Then she lets go of my hand, and I know she's back in Kazier's arms. I hear him whisper in her ear, and then I hear the soft giggle that follows.

"Someone's glaring at me right now. Don't tell me you're already taken and my chances are shot to shit," Maso's voice booms next to me.

I turn his way. "Who?"

"You didn't answer my question, Pollie."

"No. But who is staring?"

"I don't know, one of Kazier's men. Scary mother fucker if you ask me that's for sure. He looks like he's ready to walk over and rip my cock out, then hang it around his neck for good measure."

The laugh comes from nowhere, I can't help it. The shit that comes out of his mouth can only be believed when you hear it. I bet his facial expressions are the same. He doesn't seem to be a man who can hold much back.

I may have a screw loose, I think. I may even be missing a key ingredient that's needed as protection. Because I should not want to be anywhere near him. Except. I want to be.

At first, Death intrigued me. Here was this man, who couldn't remove my hand from his. Then another feeling started to stir within me. He became this man, who I felt better being around, someone who made me feel desired. Someone I wanted to be around, as much as he wanted to be around me.

Then when the knife incident occurred, it threw me. But it didn't deter me because I know he did it from fear. He wouldn't have done it otherwise. Everything he does is calculated, he thinks everything through. So when that knife paused on my neck and didn't slice, I knew he didn't think it over properly. If he did, I wouldn't be standing here, inches away from him right now. I would be in the ground, not even breathing.

So I want to know. I want to know why he did it? Why he couldn't do it? He doesn't scare me— no, it's the opposite—he intrigues me.

"That's Death," I say instantly knowing who he's talking about. Because as of right now, I can feel his penetrating stare.

"Fucking suits him. Look, no disrespect, Pollie. But I'm kind of afraid if I don't step away from you right now that my cock... I will be wearing it as a necklace sooner rather than later."

I hear his footsteps as he pushes away from me, and I feel Death as he makes his way to me. Trapping me with his presence.

CHAPTER 5

Death

I don't dream. I don't ever remember dreaming. But I have been. I've been dreaming of *her*. I wake up covered in sweat every morning, because of *her*. I don't want *her* to burden me the way she does, I want it all to go away. I figured months without seeing her would do just that, but it hasn't.

Now I can see her, standing there, in a dress that she should never wear in public.

My dreams don't do her justice.

Not one bit.

She laughs at that cockhead—I want to kill him for making her laugh. The way her eyes scrunch up and her nose crinkles in laughter, he shouldn't be making her do that, it's not his right.

I was warned not to go within close distance of her, and if I saw her to walk away. Boss made that crystal clear. Elina even made it clearer that I should not provoke. So I have stayed in the one spot for most of the evening, not even realizing that I have, in fact, been creeping closer to her. I watch as her lips move, her fingers dance along on her cane. She wants to dance, she wants to move to the music. Music is her life. I wonder when was the last time she danced, then I want to shoot myself for even thinking of something so stupid.

What the fuck do I care? But I seem too, that's the problem.

Elina's brother's eyes find mine, he holds his stare before he speaks to her, then his eyes drop away as he talks. As I edge my way slowly closer, he walks away leaving her standing there in the clutches of Elina, who's currently shaking her head at me as I step up in front of her.

"Pollie," Elina says trying to guide her away. She doesn't move and holds strong. Her eyes are on me, her body pointed toward mine. Even though I know she can't see me, it's like she can read me better than anyone else. Pollie shrugs her arm free, and her small hand reaches out for me. I look at it, and for the first time I'm afraid to take it. Because I could be so bad for her, I don't want to taint her. She's the only good in this world, and mixing it with me is a sure fire disaster.

"Death…" Her lips move, sound comes out, but I can't seem to take that step. I feel glued. I don't want to inflict pain on her, I don't want her to be tainted with my bad. She's so far from it. She takes a step forward, and her hand connects with my chest. I take a deep breath as she traces it down my arm and comes in contact with my hand. Her small fingers wrap around mine, she squeezes, and my hand does the same to hers.

We stand in the same spot, Elina's eyes are trained on us. I don't look at her, I'm not interested in what she thinks. Looking around, I notice the outdoor area is empty, so I move her with me. She almost falls over in her heels as I pull her along, but her hand lands on my back to keep herself upright. Opening the door, I observe someone standing there. I nod my head toward the door in a *'get out now'* gesture, and they basically run past us shutting the door and leaving the area empty so now there's just the two of us. I drop her hand and take a step back. She doesn't move, standing still.

"I can feel your eyes on me." Her voice is so soft, so kind. "Do you hate me?" she asks, her hand comes up and touches her neck. It lingers for a second, her finger running along the small puckered scar that's there, then she drops it to her side. "Are you going to answer me?"

"No."

Her nose scrunches up in confusion. "No, you don't hate me? Or no, you don't want to answer me?" I hear her fast intake of breath as she becomes impatient with me. I like it.

"I don't hate you."

Her arms flail around then fall back down. She mutters, "Finally," then takes a step toward me. "Why did you do it?"

No roundabout talk. She wants an answer to a question, and I have no idea what to give her.

"I don't know," is all I can manage to say.

She shakes her head. "You do. Don't lie to me. Tell me."

"Because I didn't like the feelings."

"What feelings?"

I shake my head. Why must she push? "That I was having for you."

"I want you to take me home." Her free hand pushes outward in my direction.

"Are you sure that's what you want?" I look to

her hand like it's poison. She can't seriously be asking to be alone with me when no one else is around?

"Yes. You won't hurt me again."

"You don't know that." My hand runs through my hair, she's growing some balls.

"I do. Now take me home, please." Her hand still stretched outward toward me.

I look at her face, then back at her hand. Mine inches closer, and eventually I take hold of it. Her beautiful hand instantly calms me. All my worries disappear. And I know she's right, if she has a hold of my hand, I won't hurt her. Those bad thoughts won't enter because somehow her presence stops them. Not all, just the ones where I could hurt her.

I guide her to the car. No one stops us when we leave. That is until Elina walks out and her hand pulls Pollie backward catching her off guard. I grab Pollie before she falls. Her dress is so soft.

Contact, full body contact, I shouldn't be having with her.

It makes me want to glide my hands, all over her body. I resist the urge, pulling her upright. Her scent clogs my senses. I almost forget Elina is there until she speaks.

"You can't leave with him, Pollie. I won't allow it."

Pollie straightens her spine. I don't even look to Elina, it's not her I'm worried about. Fuck. She could shoot me again and I would still come back. Can't put this fucker in the ground until I'm ready.

Pollie's hand reaches up. I almost want to snatch it back, take a hold of it. Her hands are mine. No one else's. I shake my head as I watch, trying to not think about her hands, the ones that calm me when there's even no reason to. They just...do.

Pollie's hand squeezes Elina's shoulder. "It's okay. I'll text you if I need you," Pollie speaks then turns and starts walking away. Leaving Elina standing there staring, but she doesn't stop us knowing that I'm not forcing her. She climbs in the car, and I find it's impossible to keep my eyes off her. Pollie's body is so unlike any woman I've previously fucked. Most women I fuck have fake breasts and are covered in make-up.

Pollie is just... Pollie.

Herself.

She doesn't speak as we drive back to her house. She doesn't even fidget. Instead, she just sits there, lost in her own thoughts. I don't turn the engine off as we come to a stop in front of her house, afraid of getting out of the car and having to say goodbye.

"Can you walk me in?" she asks, her hand on the handle of the car door. It takes a lot of willpower to cut the engine and climb out to go to her. She has the door open when I reach her, her right foot already out on the ground. I grab her arm to guide her, a smile touches her lips, and I close the door leading her to her apartment. I haven't actually been inside before, all the other times I've been with her, I've taken her to my house. She touches the buttons, the door buzzes and she pushes it open. I stand there. Her half inside and me still outside when she tugs at me to follow her.

"I want you to come inside," she states, walking completely through her door.

I don't argue, I don't pull away, just follow her instead. Pollie's hand is still on me as she walks with me inside. My steps are slow, but my mind is racing. I don't want to think too much, so I focus on everything and anything but my thoughts.

Her place is extensive, and open space. Just one couch sits in the living room. A kitchen as soon as you enter, and a bedroom off the living room.

I don't think she realizes she shouldn't be left

alone with me. *Where is her head at?* I did cut her throat attempting to kill her.

"Why am I here?"

She doesn't need her cane as she walks around, she moves like she knows exactly to the inch where everything is located. Everything perfectly positioned, so she can easily find her way.

"I want to know why," she simply says as she reaches her couch. She doesn't sit, but her body is still positioned facing toward me. I take a few steps so I'm closer to her. To listen to her better I tell myself when really it's just because I can't stay away from her. "I don't understand you. I understand a lot of people, it's something I have to be good at... judging people. You... I don't understand." She sits down, and I walk closer, now standing in front of her, looking down at her small frame.

"You'll never understand me."

Her head pulls up, her eyebrows scrunch. "Why?"

"Because... *I* don't even understand *me*."

"That doesn't make any sense, Death. And what's with that name? That can't be your birth name, surely. Tell me your real name?" Her voice is demanding, I've never heard her demand, ever.

"You don't want to know the meaning behind that name?"

She shakes her head, and I watch as her blonde hair shakes over her face. I instantly reach out, brushing it back. It's so soft, unlike anything I've touched. I run my fingers through it feeling the silky strands. She sits up straighter, and I drop down so I'm squatting, having no idea why. Her hand comes up. She reaches for my face, I pull away, but she insists. Her tiny hand touches my face—it's rough, I haven't shaved for days. Then before I know what I'm doing, my lips touch hers. I don't move, afraid that she'll scream or find something and stab me for touching something so good. Or possibly die on the spot for even thinking I could have someone so out of my league. Someone so.... pure.

Her mouth opens, then her lips start to move. Shock radiates through me, she's kissing me back. And before I know it, I have her by her neck and pushed back on the couch, her mouth on mine, and kissing the ever-loving shit out of her.

She doesn't push the monster away. I wonder if she's my toy? A toy put in front of me to test my limits because she does, she tests every single one of them.

CHAPTER 6

Pollie

His lips, oh my God, his lips. So full, so soft. I've never touched or kissed lips like his. It's like a sex cushion on my lips, that invades you and makes you think of dirty things. It can't be legal. His hand creeps up, it wraps around my throat and he pushes me backward, his large body encasing me.

He's large, I'm a third his size, and it should worry me because he could easily overpower me. Hell, he could easily kill me without a second thought. And he almost did, but he hesitated, he wanted them to stop him. He didn't care about himself, he craved to be stopped. Because he held that knife to my neck, but he didn't slice, and he could have so easily sliced me open.

My hands skim down his face, going to his arms. He doesn't stop kissing me, he also doesn't move his hands from my throat either. I push up on him, he groans into my mouth, then in a second he's gone. His body no longer on mine, his hands no longer touching me.

"We can't!"

I hear his footsteps as he walks to the front door, my mind still lost on his lips. My finger runs over my lips, the tingles that are present are still prickling. How did he do that?

"Stop touching your lips!" he barks at me.

He hasn't left.

His voice isn't close, but at least he's still here.

"You're an incredible kisser," I praise him.

He doesn't speak, and I worry that somehow while lost in my own thoughts that he's left, then I hear his boot hit the tiled floor as he takes a step.

"Do you want me to kill you? Is that what you're asking for?" His voice still too far away to hear him properly, so I stand and walk over to him. I hear his breathing as soon as I'm close enough. My hand reaches out and makes contact. His breathing isn't as harsh and labored as soon as I touch him.

"I think your feelings toward me confuse you," I tell him honestly. "Tell me why?"

"Because I want to kill you."

I try not to gasp because I know he speaks the truth. I can hear it in the way his voice is rough, rigid and inflexible like it was a difficult thing to say, but he had to say it because it's the truth.

"Will you kiss me again?" I dare ask. I crave his warmth, his desire, my lips want him back on me.

"No."

"Will you stay? Just sleep next to me and hold my hand?" I temp him with my words. Knowing he doesn't want to go further, but I need to know more, I want to know more.

"Do you want to wake up covered in your own blood?"

I drop my hand from his, but as soon as I do he reaches for it and takes it again. Then his phone starts ringing and he curses when he answers it. I hear rushed talking, something about Kazier, then I feel him drop my hand and click off the phone button.

"I have to go."

"Why?"

"Because my job is to clean up the mess... destroy the evidence." He doesn't walk, he's waiting for my reaction.

"What does that mean?"

"Work it out, Pollie, then you'll see who I really am. Work out what kind of mess I would have to clean up for someone like my family," he expresses harshly then walks away. I hear the door close behind him then his voice booms from on the other side of the door. "Lock it! You don't want me back after I've cleaned. Trust me."

I do as he says, my hands quickly on the door finding the lock and flicking it. Then I slide the extra lock across as a habit. Slowly I slide down, dropping to the floor. His words float around, and I try to figure out if it's as bad as I think it is.

It can't be, can it?

****

A knock wakes me from my sleep. I press my watch on my hand, and it reads out the time—two a.m. *Who would be knocking this late?* Then I remember his words, about not letting him in. I stay in bed and listen as the knocks come, a pause, then again another knock. I manage to stand next to my bed while the rapping continues. My feet are bare and the wooden flooring beneath my feet is cold. As I walk out toward the front door, his knocking is now becoming heavier, more vigorous, and soon it'll wake everyone up, not just me.

"Pollie..." His voice is dark, dangerous. My hand squeezes around the door knob, but that voice makes me stop from pulling it open.

What state is he in?

"I can hear you breathing, Pollie." He stops banging, now he's just there, standing outside my door. I know he hasn't moved, I just know he's waiting. "Open the door, Pollie."

"You told me not to." My voice squeaks, letting him know I'm unsure, scared.

"I know." He stops talking. I take a deep breath thinking that's it, then he continues, "But I want to touch you."

My head drops against the door. He didn't want me to touch him before, why does he now? What's changed?

"Will you hurt me?" I ask my hand now back on the door, waiting for his answer.

"I'll try not to." That's all he says, and I'm pretty sure that's the only answer I'm going to get. So I unlock the first lock, followed quickly by the second, then pull the door open slowly.

He doesn't move to me when the door is fully open, and he doesn't touch me at all, let alone speak. I stand at the door, then take a step back, letting him decide for himself if he wants to come inside. Then the smell assaults my senses, he smells like blood. It's a coppery, metallic smell and is hard to mistake.

When my hand touches my kitchen bench, I hear the door shut, then both locks snap into place. His footsteps come closer and his hand touches my shoulder. I try not to jump as it does, but I definitely flinch, and he notices straight away by removing his hand.

"I need to shower," is all he says. His footsteps retreat as he walks away. I hear my bathroom door open, and I walk into my bedroom. Lying back onto my bed, I wonder if it was the right thing to do—to let him inside my home.

He doesn't take long to shower, and soon after, I feel my bed dip when he gets into it next to me. His body heat suffocates me as I feel it emanating from him. His hand touches one of mine that's lying on the bed next to me. He doesn't squeeze or grip it hard he just holds my hand softly.

I turn my body toward him, my free hand reaches over to touch him, and I come into contact with bare skin. "Do you have clothes on?" I ask pulling my hand back slightly, but he holds on tighter.

"No," he replies. I hear his breathing becoming heavier, mine matching his. My legs squeeze tighter, I want him. I think I have for a long time. The only reason I haven't pushed is that a part of me is scared of what I don't know about him.

"Will you kiss me?" I ask.

He lets go of my hand, I feel the bed dip as he moves. His hands go to either side of my body, just below my head and his body touches mine. He's hard and directly on me, his cock touches my pussy. I try my hardest not to squeeze. Not to let him know how turned on I am, when his mouth latches onto mine.

He tastes sweet, so divine. I can't help myself when my hands go up, and lock onto his back—his naked back. I run my hands down, touching his waist, where his pants should be, but aren't. He pushes himself onto me. A moan leaves my mouth, but his lips don't leave me for a second. His tongue dances with mine. His lips full, soft but firm at the same time. He lifts a hand while kissing me, and it goes between us. His hand slips into my panties, and I automatically arch from his touch, even though his body still covers mine. I know I'm wet, and I know any second now he'll know as well.

His hand dips lower and he touches my clit. My tongue stops moving, my mouth opens wide. He flicks it hard with his finger, then rubs my wetness all over as he slips his finger into me. He keeps on kissing even though I keep stopping from his fingers distracting me.

Then as if time stands still he stops, and I feel the air whoosh over me as he pushed up from the bed and leaves me. It takes me a moment before I realize he's completely off the bed while I lay there panting and wanting more.

"Why did you stop?" I ask, knowing he's still in the room. Sensing his presence, I can hear his breathing even if it's not as heavy as mine.

"You wouldn't like it."

I sit up, confused. *What does he mean by that?*

"I'm pretty sure I would," I tell him, my voice firm. My legs tightly clamped together.

"You wouldn't, and it *would* scare you."

"It's just sex, Death."

I hear him moving around then listen to him getting dressed and it makes me mad.

"It's not! Don't answer your door again if I'm there... or next time, I won't stop."

"I will," I shout at him as he walks away.

He doesn't respond, and all that I hear is the door slamming as he leaves.

CHAPTER 7

Death

Past, Eighteen years old.

I remember the first body that was solely mine. I remember how it was dropped onto my floor like it didn't mean a thing. I guess it didn't, but it did to me. That death, all death, meant a lot to me. It was the only constant. The only thing I knew I could trust in this life. There was always death, and I never doubted that there wouldn't be. It was reliable. Unlike people. Kazier walked in after the men dropped the body off, his nose scrunched up when he looked down at the mangled heap of skin and bones. He liked the killing, loved it actually, just not the aftermath. That was why I was there.

"You just going to leave it there?" he asked pointing to the body.

I shrugged my shoulders. One thing that had

never bothered me was a dead body. It was always so peaceful, so serene. I was fixated from an early age. I blame the lack of a father, and my only brother always doing the dirty work for Kazier's father. A dead body was something I saw daily from the age of ten. To me, it was nothing. Just like another piece of furniture scattered around the house. I remembered saying that to Kazier once, and the look he gave me, I realized at that moment that possibly I wasn't normal.

But what was normal within our family anyway?

I'd just purchased the house, it was the second time he'd come to visit me. I didn't like him. Hell, I didn't like anyone. But I did, however, respect the fuck out of him. He was bringing meaning back to our name. He didn't treat us as dogs the way his father did, the way my father did. Technically, his father was still our Pakhan, but he didn't act as if he was, leaving it all to Kazier.

"You ever get sick of it?" he asked as he watched me pick up the body. I lifted it over my shoulder—it was still moveable. Obviously the guy hadn't been dead too long.

"Sick of what?" He nodded toward the body. "It's what I know. You ever get sick of the blood or the killings?" I asked him, and he shook his head. I knew he didn't, I saw him once after a killing, his hand kept on touching the blood, he was intrigued with it. I wanted to tell him then about my fascination for blood, but in an entirely different way, with a woman involved. Then I shook it off and took the body away.

"I heard you have a fascination with blood. The rumors true?" he asked, tapping his knuckles on the door.

"Why are you here, Kazier?" I asked him as I dropped the body. I didn't want to answer his question. He didn't need to know. Even though I wasn't ashamed of it, I just preferred to not share my life.

"Your brother called me, said you've been ignoring him. Wanted me to check that you were still alive."

I waved my hands around, showing I was indeed alive. "You can go now," I said picking the body back up.

He shook his head and tapped my shoulder as he walked out the front door, without another word.

I walked downstairs to the basement. It was so silent that I could feel a headache coming on. I hung *the body up, cutting in multiple places, draining as much blood as possible. I usually let it hang for a day, but that day I didn't have any patience. I cut, and cut until enough blood had been drained so I could start the final process—the cutting. As soon as I had the guy on the table, I turned my music on and cranked it as loud as it would go. Heavy metal music exploded through the room, echoing off the stone walls. The room was full of barrels and glass bottles of acid laced the shelves at the back of the room.*

To some, this was the worst part. Most men couldn't handle this. Not just the disposal, but the smell. The smell hit you as soon as you walked into this room. It was potent, and if you weren't used to it, it could take your breath away. Viktor once tried carrying a body in here with me one night, but he dropped it as soon as I opened the door and walked as far away as quickly as he possibly could.

I bleed my dead bodies out. First, they're hung up on a hook, then my surgical knife cuts all major arteries, draining them of all their blood. Then I start off with a saw, removing the legs from the torso. It was always the easiest way to dispose of the body. Trying to place the whole body in a barrel of acid was tricky, and usually ended up with acid everywhere. This why this room has been built to my purpose—drains coat the floor, ventilation is everywhere.

I wore protective clothing and haven't once had acid touch my skin—though the possibility of doing that was ever present—even a gas mask covers my face. Not all my skin is protected. It could easily hit me if I weren't careful enough. The music helps me with that, helps me concentrate and block out the world. The whole process calms me, it's the only place I can go without judgment. I see the way people look and stare at me. I know I'm not average, my face is hard, and I don't smile. I have ink, piercings, and look like I just stepped out from a lifetime jail sentence.

People don't trust what makes them uncomfortable—I make them uncomfortable.

I applied pressure, cutting in deeper. I felt the first bone and utilized more force cutting with the saw. I haven't tried using an electric saw. I suppose that would be faster, but would probably use more power. I preferred my small hand saw, I desired the distraction, and the lost time it gave me.

The bone snapped as I sawed through the last part. Then I pulled the first leg free, like snapping a drumstick from a chicken. I could feel the sweat dripping down my face, and watched as it dripped onto the body below. It didn't stop me, it made me keep going, pushed me further. A high took over me, a thrilling feeling. The music pumped through my ears, and I got to work on the arms, tearing limb from limb. I didn't have a clock down there, and I never heard when someone came to the door. It was the way I liked it, I preferred to not be interrupted. That was why this house was perfect, the basement was like my own person purpose built dungeon.

The torso laid by itself, the legs and arms now detached from the body. The guy was in his late thirties, I suspected a smoker as well. As I opened up his stomach and sliced through his insides, his lungs were partially black. In some cases, if the body were very fresh, I would store certain body parts for Kazier to sell on the black market—kidneys being his favorite.

This body, however, I couldn't do that with. I'd left it too long, and nothing was viable. As I tore his stomach out, I dropped it straight into the barrel of acid. It sizzled as it entered, then disappeared. I removed everything else my hand touched, not bothered by the care I took. Let's face it he was dead anyway. And I liked the way it felt in my hand, the way the bowels were soft and squishy, the heart tender but also tough. Once I did that, I placed his legs into the barrel, making sure my mask and gloves were on. The bigger the body parts, the bigger the splash it made. His arms went in next, then the torso.

I removed my gloves and mask and took a step back. I could see the acid slowly eating away at the skin, making its way through the flesh. Then eventually it would destroy the bones as well. I once tried this in a bathtub, needless to say, I lost the bath and some of the floor was etched away. Glass lined barrels became my choice, and to this day they haven't disappointed.

I leave the body in the barrel for up to three days before I call in a clean-up crew, and request a new barrel. By the time they empty it, nothing was left of the body. Wouldn't faze me if there was.

The basement's fully vented. It was one of the building requirements that were instigated after I'd bought the house. It had to be fitted out with all the necessary requirements that were needed to keep the area from being detected. The smell was so strong, that if it wasn't properly vented, you'd never be able to step foot in the basement again without serious physical injury. The venting system runs through washers and a cleaning system, so by the time it hits the atmosphere there's no detectable smell.

I made my way up the stairs, and as I did, my phone started ringing—my brother. He was the only one that called. Sometimes I went weeks without speaking to him, sometimes he called every day when it was particularly hard for him. I didn't understand that part, he said it was easier over there. That here with me was not liveable, but it was never easy, least of all for him. I don't understand it, at all, and think that he calls because he thinks I will.

I did the same thing after all. The only difference—I enjoy it.

Some preferred to read, watch movies, I preferred death, it was as simple as that. It was my escape, forever, or how long it would take me.

CHAPTER 8

Pollie

Present

He left, yet again. What does he mean I wouldn't like it? I'm pretty sure I would like him touching me. Actually, I know I would. He's left me in a daze.

The next day, my notes are off, my distraction overtaking me.

What has he done to me?

Is it because I need sex?

I didn't think I was that kind of girl. I've gone ages without it, never craving it. I'm an easy going person, I don't need things. Certain things I can live without, and I thought sex was one of them. I guess I was wrong, and I'm trying to convince myself otherwise. But now all I can think about is my hands on his skin. His smooth skin. My hands running up and down his toned body. His fingers between my legs, his mouth on mine. I want more.

The class finishes up, and people begin to say their goodbyes. I don't even know if I've replied appropriately to them. I start walking out—every step harder than the last one—and make my way to the driver that's waiting for me.

He greets me with a "Hello," and I give him an address. It's not mine, though. He doesn't question me, and before I know it the driver stops because we've arrived.

"We're here, Miss." His voice breaks through my sexual thoughts. My mind so preoccupied, I didn't even realize we'd moved.

His hands.

His mouth.

"Thank you," I reply feeling for the door handle and opening it.

"Should I wait, Miss?" he asks.

I think about it, I should say yes, in case he doesn't want to see me. Instead, I go against my better judgment and tell him no. I feel my legs begin to tremble when I climb his steps. I shouldn't be here, I know I shouldn't. I can't help myself. *Why must I be here? Why can't I leave well enough alone?* I have a weird desire to be around him like he needs me as much as I need him. Maybe he needs more. I don't know.

My hand comes up to knock, my knuckles rapping on the door. I repeat it several times, with no answer. Just as I'm about to give up, footsteps come up behind me. I drop my hand and take a step back.

"He won't hear you." Kazier's voice comes from behind me.

I turn toward his voice. "Why?"

"He's working. He never hears anyone," he says it like I should know.

I hear Kazier push a key into the lock, then he pushes the door open.

"You coming?" he asks me.

My head drops and I wonder if I should go in, especially if he's working. Do I want to interrupt that? "He's working, he may not want to see me. I don't want to disturb him." I turn to leave when his voice stops me.

"Come in, Pollie, don't stray away. If you want

to be with him, you're going to have to accept him."

What does he mean by that?

"I do accept him," I say walking toward the door. As soon as I enter the familiar smell that encases this house takes over. I don't know exactly what it is, and a part of me doesn't want to know.

"Stay here..." Kazier's voice pauses, "...I'll go get him."

His reaction makes me wonder why I shouldn't move. Why he insisted I stay here.

I sit on his couch, music blares loudly, then it stops. Footsteps are heard coming closer shortly afterward as I hear Kazier speaking to Death, and when they both reach me, no one speaks. My fingers run up and down the top part of my cane. All thoughts I had of him earlier now vanished. Now I'm filled with... wonder.

I want to know more.

I know I do.

"Elina misses you," Kazier says, his voice is close. "I'll tell her you do as well." Then his footsteps disappear leaving me sitting in the room which is deathly quiet and I feel like I'm by myself, but I know I'm not. I can feel his stare on me. And the smell... the smell matches him, Death.

I sit in an uncomfortable silence, neither of us speaking. A million thoughts start to run rampant through my head.

Is he right for me?

Is he wrong for me?

Should I be here?

Why won't he speak to me?

Why won't he touch me?

And most of all, why do I like him so much without even knowing him?

"You left," I say breaking the silence. I hear his steps as he comes closer, his hand touches mine.

"I need to shower," he says pulling me up by my hand. At first, I think that means he wants me to leave. Instead, he doesn't let go, he keeps hold of it and pulls me in the direction opposite to the door. "Steps," he says letting me know we're walking upward.

I've never been around his house. I always stayed in the doorway, or in his living room. My fingers run along the railing as we walk up, he stops at the top and turns right. Then I hear him turn a handle and push the door open. I'm instantly met with his smell. The one that clings to him, not the one that he has after working. It's still a dense smell, like a murky musk. But it's masculine, I can't explain it. I always recognize it, and I love the sensations it brings me. I could sleep with that smell, day in and day out, and never get sick of it. He walks me over to his bed, I feel the edge hit my legs. He drops my hand and walks away, I hear the shower turn on. I sit on the bed, thoughts screaming in my head. Lost in time, I hear his footsteps pad toward me and my hand goes up when I know he's standing in front of me coming into contact with his bare skin.

"Why did you leave?"

"I can't have conventional sex."

My eyebrows scrunch in confusion. What the hell does he mean by that? "Sex is sex, right?"

"Not to me, it isn't."

My hand starts to drop lower, they run over the edges of his well-defined body.

"Can you attempt conventional with me?"

His hand touches my hip, he squeezes tightly. I can feel him contemplating the idea. "I don't do conventional. And you… well, you wouldn't like *my conventional*." He stops as his breath comes to my ear. "You're too good for my kind of regular. I'd ruin you."

I become still, my hand stops just above his waistline.

"Try my regular?" I ask lifting my other hand. I don't understand his regular, I don't even know what he means by that. I want to ask, but something inside me stops the question. I know I want him, I know I do. So I'm hoping he wants me just as badly. He wouldn't let me be here if that wasn't true. Would he?

His hand lifts from my hip, his fingers clutch my shirt and he pulls it upward. I raise my hands so he can, and in an instant, my shirt is gone. Then his hands work on my pants, he pulls them down and I step out of them, then all I have left on is my underwear. I move my hands to unclasp my bra, letting it drop to meet the pile of clothing on the floor. Then my panties, and now I stand in front of him, the sound of the water from the shower the only noise coming between us. My hand lifts again, wanting to make sure he's still there. He's gone silent. I touch his chest again, he hasn't moved, his breathing coming in small pants.

"I've seen a lot of bodies in my time, but none are as perfect as yours. That should worry you being with me."

I don't have time to question what he means by that because his hands come to my ass, and he grips my cheeks hard as he lifts me up so effortlessly. I want to know exactly what he looks like, I want to feel his facial expressions. I've never wanted to see something as bad in my life as I want to see him right now. I want to understand him, and I don't. That troubles me more than anything he's hiding from me.

I hear a door squeak open. The warm water touches my back first, his mouth comes down onto my neck next. I let my neck drop backward, my hands find his face. I pull him away from my neck and feel the edges of his face. His forehead is set with worry, crinkle lines cross deeply. I would never have guessed Death to be someone who worries.

"Tell me what you see?" I whisper dropping my mouth to his. I kiss his lips softly, I can feel him, hard just below my ass.

"I see someone who shouldn't be on this earth. I see someone, who's too good, that doesn't belong here." He lifts me again with his hands, like I'm a doll, then pulls me down hard. No warning, no warm up. A scream rips through me, his mouth tries to shut that scream up with his lips. There's pain, then the pleasure of that one action sends shots of electricity through my body. He doesn't move me straight away. He's large, larger than my ex. His cock is hitting everything, and I'm afraid if I move, the pain will be stronger. His words float straight through me, he's made me forget it all with that one action. Those fucked up words he just spoke, ones that I know hold meaning to him, ones that I know I won't truly understand or even get an answer to. "Are you hurting?" he asks me, lifting his mouth from mine, his lips still just touching mine.

"Yes," I answer. Even with the pleasure, the pain is still there.

His lips curve up, I can feel them, and then he starts to move me slower than before. It takes me a moment to adjust, and when I do, I feel my eyes become larger—the pain is completely gone. He moves me faster, deeper, harder. Before I know it, pleasure rips through me, so fast, that I don't know how to handle it. When I've had sex before, it was always on a bed, never have I had sex standing up and never have I been this turned on without even knowing I was.

"Bite me," his words are dark, I almost don't recognize that voice. "Bite me," he says again, lifting his shoulder up to me. My mouth closes over the top of his shoulder, and my teeth sink in, not too hard, just enough to leave a mark. With that he picks up speed, bouncing me harder, I have to stop myself from lifting my head and screaming. I can feel the build-up, it's almost there, so fast, and I'm so not used to it.

"Harder," he says. My teeth etch into his skin. He repeats it again, "Harder."

I bite, hard.

Breaking his skin.

I can taste blood as it touches my mouth. He feels it to because he smacks my ass hard. He likes it—a lot.

My head lifts, I kiss his mouth, my hands find his jaw, grabbing him to me. Blood is on my tongue, I don't notice until he moans into my mouth, kissing and fucking me even harder. Then I drop, my head pulls backward, straight under the water, and my body starts to shake.

Is this that big O girls talk about?

I've never experienced it, and I want more.

He isn't finished though, he keeps rocking into me, not stopping. His hand reaches down and touches my clit, making me shoot back up to the position we were just in. My legs wrap tighter around him, and before I know it, another one hits me and my hands and legs go slack. I don't know if he comes, my mind is too blank. All I know is that he carries me out, and before I know it, my eyes are closed.

CHAPTER 9

Death

I have an unhealthy obsession—you know it, I know it. She didn't know it. I guess that was the problem. She didn't know it, she couldn't see it. To others, I was in the category of evil even dangerous. But I was so much more, way more.

I'm not a person to have feelings for others—I have respect, and non-respect. Then there were other categories like love, affection, they just don't appear on my radar. I don't understand those words. So when I look down at her sleeping form, I wonder exactly what it is that I feel for her. I still didn't know.

The sex was incredible, and I didn't expect it to be. There has been only one way for me to get off, and it was not ordinary. So to have conventional sex, left me standing naked, looking down at someone who I don't quite understand, let alone explain my feelings for her.

My phone lights up on the nightstand next to her head. Her body shines brighter from the light of it. How could someone so perfect, be laying *alive* in my bed right now? Who just had my cock buried so deep inside her, and still close her eyes like she's safe.

Was she safe? I wasn't so sure.

I don't want to answer the phone. I know it's Kazier or one of the boys. I prefer standing here, exactly where I am, watching her. Watching her chest rise and fall, her tits going up and down with each breath. If she could see me, if she woke up, she'd be scared. I know that for sure.

"Yes," I breathe into the phone, trying not to speak too loudly so as to wake her up. She doesn't even stir. My hands beg to touch her, so I run my fingers down between her breasts. She moves slightly, her hand coming up to mine, touching my hand then breathing again normally. Back to sleep.

"You need to come now. I'm texting you the address. Bring your gun," Viktor says into the phone hanging up on me. I lift my hand then place it back on her skin. It's too soft to be real. I needed to mark it with my hands in the shower while I fucked her, and made her bite me, *hard*. I needed more from her, wanted more from her. She partially understood, her teeth marks still have a slight sting on my shoulder every time I move it. *Now if only I can train her to do more.* I don't bother covering her as I get dressed, I want to come home to her exactly the way she is right now—naked and helpless in my bed. Just the way I want her.

****

When I arrive, Kazier's black truck is parked on the street, with another black truck parked behind his. I climb out and walk straight to him. In the front seat is Anton, he smirks at me and taps Kazier's shoulder to gain his attention.

"Loverboy is here," Anton teases. He's so fucking annoying, like a teenage boy you want to backhand across the fucking face just for the sheer fun of it. I ignore his comment, and focus on Kazier, he turns away from me and nods his head to the apartment across from his car.

"They're selling my shit. Trying to sell higher, and killing our middle men." I look again, the house is dark. Just as I'm about to reply, footsteps come up from behind me. Freya, Kazier's ex-fiancée, and Viktor stand behind me. I look to her, wondering what the fuck she's doing here, she looks away from my eyes fast. Viktor holds his smirk, his lips fight the twitch.

"Why is she here?" I direct my question to Kazier. Anton pokes his head out of the car and looks to Freya then pops his head back in.

"She followed them. She thinks she wants to be us."

"I do not, you fuckhead. And watch your mouth. We can see who's faster at cutting each other's throat."

Viktor's head drops and he shakes his head. Anton laughs at her outburst. I look at her with hard eyes, wondering what the fuck she's talking about.

"Tell her to leave, I don't like her." It's partially true, I don't like anyone. Not even sure about how I feel toward a woman that's in my bed right now. She has my feelings so fucked up. I should have slit her throat when I had the chance.

"You can't tell me to leave," she pipes up. She looks from me to the men around us, and no one says anything. "You can't," she says making herself believe it.

"You leave, or I leave."

"Leave, Freya," Kazier says.

I watch as her face becomes red. Viktor's hand comes up to rest on her back, and she slaps it away.

She doesn't say anything as she stomps off and climbs back into the car behind Kazier's and drives away, giving us the finger when she drives by, making Anton bend over pissing himself laughing.

"Do you know how hard I've tried to get rid of her these last few days? She doesn't want to stay home." He rolls his eyes. "She doesn't want to be around this fuck." He thumbs at Kazier to which Kazier hits him in return. "All she wants to do is annoy me and this slum who's keen as a biscuit for her." He points to Viktor, but Viktor doesn't say a word. I guess he's used to Anton's rambling shit.

Kazier steps out of the car, walking around to where we are. Anton follows suit sliding out as well. Kazier looks across the road, and a light comes on then quickly turns off.

"Alive or dead?" I ask him.

Anton shakes his head. "You want everyone dead. Alive, dickhead," he replies walking ahead of us.

I stand there and wait for Kazier's words. He is, after all, the only one I take orders from.

"Preferably alive, I'll need them to make the money back they've stolen. But if they piss you off..." he stops talking and looks to me, "...scratch that. I think everyone pisses you off. If they piss me off, kill them," he says nodding his head and walking toward Anton who's already halfway across the street. Viktor walks with us, and just before we reach the stairs the door opens, and Anton pulls out two guns, holds them up to the face of the person who answered the door and the other one is pointed to the door that's half opened.

"Tell him to move, or I'll kill him," Anton directs. The man at the door nods his head toward them behind the door, and another man steps out from behind it. The guys look at both of us, taking us in then taking a step back letting Anton step inside. Guns are still raised at both their heads. We take the steps slowly and the men back further inside as we follow. Viktor walks straight past them and begins to move around the house. My job is to make sure nothing happens to Kazier. I am, after all, here to make sure he stays alive. If I fail, I'll probably be joining him in whatever hell he ends up in.

Viktor ends up walking out gripping a man by his shirt, the guy's eyes widen when they see what else he's holding—kilos of cocaine—which is obviously not theirs. Kazier walks to him and yanks it from his grasp, splits the bag open with a knife and tastes it. He stays silent for a second before he turns the knife and points it to the now three men.

They don't look too scared, which surprises me, for all they know we could kill them at any second. Instead, they look relaxed, as if they're thinking if we haven't killed them yet, why would we do it now. Wrong, one improper fidget and a bullet will go straight between his eyes.

The night before, Kazier restocked the black market with kidneys, lungs, eyes, and other body parts. His victims were users that had been avoiding paying him. They had their warnings, reached their limits, so payment was to be made one way or another. And unfortunately for them, but not for me, their price was death. And I was the bringer of it, after killing both, I ended back up on Pollie's doorstep.

She shouldn't have opened the door as I was on a massive high and hookers are my usual go to. But I knew where she was, and I wanted her, like the night calls for the darkness, she was it. I don't know how I managed to walk out, I don't know how I didn't tie her to the bed and do everything I wanted to do the minute I saw her.

"This isn't yours," Kazier says snapping my mind from thoughts of Pollie. She clogs my head more times than I want.

The man looks to the drugs in his hand, then

back at him. "Yes, they are."

Kazier nods his head to Viktor, who walks up to the man that spoke and places his knife straight in his eye. He drops, his friends jump backward away from their fallen friend, and even further away from us.

"Now you know I'm not joking when I ask a question. So tell me... where did you get this?"

The two men look at each other, afraid to speak.

One punches the other in the arm. "Tell him, man, I'm not dying because of this shit."

All eyes go the man that obviously knows. He fidgets with his hands before he speaks, "Alastair said it was easy money. All we had to do was rob a few street guys. So we did." He shrugs his shoulders.

"You stole from me, from the Smirnov."

Their eyes widen at the name, they know it well. Everyone with a pulse in this city knows the name.

"We... we d-didn't... m-mean to. We d-didn't... k-know," one man stutters as he speaks.

"I'm in a considerably nice mood, possibly

because I just got my cock sucked. So, you have twelve hours to make up for my losses."

"We can't! We don't have that kind of money."

Kazier looks back to me, I pull my gun out, and the man starts screaming.

"No. No. We can do it."

"If you don't, there's only one way I can get my money back, and that's by the hands of this man." Kazier nods to me. "Trust me when I say, sell your soul first before you meet the end of his knife." He turns and walks out.

Anton keeps his gun raised as we walk out, smirking at the men.

"You don't want that man's hands anywhere on you. So I would hurry," he says following us out.

CHAPTER 10

Pollie

I wake in a bed I'm not familiar with, but the smell I know. I sit up and knows it's late. The door closes downstairs then the stomping of boots begin to move up toward me. I touch next to me to see if he's there, and he's not. The door creaks open, and I instantly know it's him. It's then I realize I'm naked, completely naked without even a sheet covering me. My skin breaks out in goosebumps.

"Did you leave?" I ask him.

He hasn't moved. I know he's there. I don't know how exactly, just that his presence is so intense I can feel it anywhere. His breathing is quiet and I have excellent hearing, so for me to not be able to hear him, it scares me.

"Yes," he replies. I hear the ruffling of clothes, then him stepping closer to me. His fingers touch my skin and he lifts my chin so I'm looking upward.

"I'm going to fuck you again, with your conventional."

A shiver breaks out over my skin. That wasn't my kind of conventional, but I won't tell him differently, because even if I didn't know it, I still loved it despite my better judgment. I nod my head in his hands, his fingers scroll downward, going over my breast. He stops on my left breast and twists my nipple in his fingers, making a spark down below that I didn't know could happen from a simple touch. His touch is hard, nowhere near gentle. I don't think he knows how to be gentle, even when he holds my hand, he holds it like I may run away at any minute.

"Am I staying?" I ask as his fingers travel lower, going down below. He doesn't answer me straight away, just keeps up his torture. He reaches my clit, strokes it with his finger, dipping it in then bringing it out to rub over my clit again. Then he pinches it with the same force he just used on my nipple. I jump backward, but he holds me in place with a hand to my thigh.

"Yes, don't think about leaving." His voice sounds dangerous, and I wonder if it's only because he's ready and wants to fuck.

A part of me says no, that I should be scared

because he's not talking about that, he plans to keep me. Whether I like it or not.

He grabs the back of my knees, pushes them up and placing me on my back. Then he spreads me wide. I feel exposed. What does he see when he looks down there, is it disgusting? Then I have my answer when his mouth lands, he does one long stroke from bottom to top with his tongue, making me quiver with my legs still up in the air. He repeats it, another long stroke, then he's gone, leaving me open and wanting more.

I try to sit up, but he won't allow it. His hands hold my legs firmly in place. I wait for him to speak, to let me know what's going on, but not a word leaves his mouth. I can feel the build-up, no one moves, we're both locked in place. Then it happens again, he slams into me, without any warning, completely taking me by surprise. I scream again, my hand flies up to cover my mouth.

I've never screamed so much during sex.

Am I a screamer now?

Or is it just him that makes me scream, with his brutal yet off the charts sex? A part of me wants to know what he means when he says this is not his conventional. I want to know what makes him think this is normal. And how this isn't to him. It excited me, yet scares me all at the same time.

My back arches upward like it has a mind of its own. His body comes forward, I can feel him hovering over me. Then his hand is in my hair, he pulls it hard, I'm pretty sure I can hear the snap of my own hair with each pull. I reach for his hands, untangling them, pulling my hair free. He doesn't say anything so I drag him down to me for a kiss. He lets me, and his thrusts become not so rough— almost, almost, normal.

I know it won't last long. Before I can crave more of his kisses, he bites my lip, then his hands are under me picking me up with him still inside of me. Then I'm turned and slammed into a wall. Pain shoots through my back the moment it happens. It makes me dizzy, as my head hits far too hard. His hands start moving me up and down, up and down. I can't keep up, I don't even bother keeping up before my next thought leaves my brain. I scream again, louder than before.

He holds me with one hand, pushes my head down to his shoulder. "Bite, hard!"

I do as he says, while the orgasm rips through me. I need to let it out, so I don't think twice this time when my teeth sink severely into the opposite shoulder from the one I bit last time. He now moves me with his hips alone, pushing me up and down, then I feel him shake at the same time I'm coming down from it, and I know he came. He holds me for a second longer before he drops me on the bed lying down next to me, naked.

It takes me longer than normal to catch my breath, to come back down from the high. When I do, I reach for him and feel warm liquid on his shoulder. I instantly sit up, scrambling my way closer to him. I climb onto his stomach, touching him all over his chest, then to both shoulders—one is bleeding, and the other is raised.

"I did this?" I ask touching it softly, so as to not hurt him.

"Yes," he says.

I cover my mouth with my hands, his hands don't touch me as I sit on him.

"Oh my God, why didn't you tell me to stop?" When he doesn't answer me at first, I hit his chest with my palm for an answer.

"Because I like it."

That answer takes me aback. "You like to be hurt?" I ask him confused. "Or bleed?"

"Both," he tells me.

I shake my head not understanding. "You want to do this to me?" I ask him. "When we have sex?"

His hands comes up and touches my belly, he runs it along my skin. "I've wanted to, yes."

"Now you don't?" I ask him because he's not giving me straight answers.

"No."

"Why?"

I hear him sigh. "Perfection shouldn't be marred, not on the outside anyway."

I have no words in answer to that. None what-so-ever. I don't understand what that even means. I want to ask, but I have a feeling I would only get a one-word answer. I lay my head on his chest above his heart. His hands move away from me, I feel them on my side but not moving. I reach for them and place them on my back, one by one.

"It's cuddling, I like to cuddle."

"You do this often?" he asks clearly interested.

"Not often enough, though I do like it right here. You're so warm, I could lay here 'til I die."

His hand stills, it was moving slightly just circling one spot on my back, but now his body is rigid.

"Do you want to die by my hand?"

Now it's my turn to go rigid. I don't move, too afraid of what's to come. I still don't understand him.

"No. Promise me you won't hurt me again?"

"I don't make promises I can't keep," he replies then starts the motion again of circling my back.

CHAPTER 11

Death

Sex with Pollie, it's my new favorite hobby. I don't want to stop. I don't want to let her go. I've fucked her twice this morning. My body proves it with the marks she's left on my skin, each and every one I crave more than the next. I watch as she walks down the stairs fully dressed, her hair fans over her shoulders, the clothes what she wore from the day before. I locked us in my bedroom so I could have her body. She smiles when she walks down. I don't know how, but she always seems to know where I am. It's like she's attuned to me, and that can't happen. We are two opposites—she's too good, and I'm too bad.

"Can you call me a cab?" she asks in the sweetest possible voice I've ever heard.

I close my eyes and take a deep breath, trying to control myself from grabbing her and tying her to the bed, so she can never leave me.

"I'll drive you," I manage to say instead.

She nods her head, and I walk closer but not touching her. She puts out her hand, letting it dangle in front of me. She knows I want to take it. I like to take her hand in mine. It feels, odd, but yet good. I'm still trying to understand that emotion.

I take it, and we walk to the car. She climbs in, and I watch her ass as she does, not even caring if she knows I'm leering.

****

Her hand pauses on the door when we come to a stop, sunglasses cover half of her face, and she turns to lean toward me. Her hand touches my cheek, she comes in even closer, then her lips touch mine. I don't move, and she soon realizes this and pulls away. Not saying goodbye as she gets out of the car, I drive a block down the street, enough so I can still see her. I watch as she stands on the sidewalk in front of her building, doing nothing at all. I sit there and wait and watch as she eventually walks inside, shutting the door behind her.

"Death," I hear coming through my car blue-tooth. I didn't look when I answered, I was too busy watching her. Now I'm sitting, staring at an empty space where she once was. "You twisted homo bastard, answer me you fucktard."

I shake my head, his vocabulary sometimes amazes me.

"I have a pineapple. You reckon I can stick that in your ass and make you call me daddy?" Anton's voice booms through. I hear background noise and his laugh as someone takes the phone away from him.

"Death. Boy's night. Be here at nine," Kazier says hanging up. I hear the smack he delivers and Anton's laughing voice in the background before the click.

Boys' night? What the actual fuck!

I don't do boys' nights.

I don't do any nights unless it involves tearing someone apart.

I drive straight back to my house, trying to push her from my mind, and the only thing that does that fully is being locked away in my basement. When I arrive I can smell her, her scent is everywhere. Like she's never left. Like she's been here for days on end.

I walk over to the door that lets me lock everything away. It's a heavy steel door, and it only unlocks with my hand. If I'm downstairs I usually just leave it unlocked. The only people that come here is Kazier and the body movers. But when I'm not, the door is locked, and no one can enter unless they have my hand.

I walk down the stairs, darkness takes over. I switch on the red fluorescent light making everything take on a tinge of red. One table is bare when I walk down, the other holds a woman. She would have been beautiful alive, I would have paid to fuck her. Her tits are perfect, her hair is long and runs down the sides of her arm, and her body toned. I don't care for the reasons behind their deaths. I have a job, I don't ask questions I don't want answers to. Bodies show up, and it's my job to dispose of them.

Kazier wants me to train someone else and consider being by his side more than I already am. I don't know how I feel about that. I don't think I want to, I'd miss this too much. The way the saw slices through the first layer of skin, the way the arms drop from her body as soon as that final push is delivered through her bones, excites me. The next arm is exactly the same. Her hair lays there, looking naked now with no arms to hide the darkness that's in it. I brush my fingers through it, to feel the softness. Ultimately, I compare it to Pollie's, and it doesn't measure up. The color is dark, compared to her lightness. It feels soft, whereas Pollie's feels like silk.

I make my first mistake—with Pollie on my mind—as I drop the arm in the barrel of acid. I'm not entirely covered, drops spring up and one lands on my shirt burning straight through to my skin. I immediately wipe it off, but the burning continues. I pull my shirt off, tossing it to the floor and race over to the clean-up station.

The tattoo on my arm is now red and raw as I pour bleach over it and then scrub with soap and water. I look back to the dead woman wanting to cut her even more for making me make a mistake, for making me think of Pollie and comparing them. I flick the music off, turn the lights out, and go back upstairs.

I check the time—almost eight. How do I lose so many hours? I don't even know how time disappears on me.

Usually, I'd walk in at night time, then walk out when the sun is rising in the morning on a busy night and have no idea where the time went.

****

When I arrive at Kazier's later on, Viktor answers the door. He doesn't speak as he pushes it open and walks in. I stand there for a second, hearing Anton's laughter echo from inside and mentally prepare myself not to kill him. He *is* family after all. To some, that means a lot.

Kazier's voice booms out with my name. When I walk in, they're on the back patio, the same one I wanted to cut Pollie's throat on, the same one I almost died on afterward. Anton smiles holding up a bottle of vodka, Kazier waves me over. Between them, on the table, sits at least ten bottles of vodka, some opened, some still closed. I take a seat, and Kazier hands me a bottle, I look at it and shake my head. His eyebrows scrunch in question. He doesn't ask, but Anton does instead.

"You don't want to drink with us, pretty boy?" he asks placing the bottle to his lips, taking a long sip then wiping the excess away with the back of his hand as he stares at me.

"I don't drink," I reply. I've never taken a drink, I've never wanted to. I've got enough fucked morals, I don't want to add addiction to my fucked up mess. His head drops down between his legs as he laughs, Viktor shakes his head.

"Well, now's the time you do. Sit down you hunk of junk."

I think I may have to drink, to be able to put up with Anton. Because killing him is not an option.

Well, not right now anyway while everyone's around. Kazier holds a bottle out to me, tips his head toward it and I take it.

"Always vodka," I say more to myself.

"We are Russian, dickhead. It's our drink," Anton replies.

I place the bottle to my lips, it burns when I take it down. Holding back the cough that wants to force its way up I take another, the more you drink, the more the burn disappears.

"I wouldn't recommend drinking the whole bottle on your first time," Viktor says. I hold it up and see I've already drunk half of it, two long chugs and it'll be gone.

"Where's your woman?" I ask looking around, I'm sure she wants to put another bullet in me. The first one didn't finish me off.

"With Pollie, girls' night or some shit," Kazier says placing the bottle to his lips. He starts shuffling a deck of cards. I stand and instantly feel the effects. Her name makes me want to leave, just the sound of it makes me want to go where she is. I sit back down, and no one says a word. Kazier eyes me quickly, then continues to shuffle.

"Why are we here?" Viktor slaps my back with

his hand, clearly having drunk too much.

"Buck's night," he says nodding toward Kazier. Kazier doesn't look up from the cards, that I'm sure have been well over-shuffled.

"Why isn't there hookers?" I ask looking around.

"Because he doesn't want to lose his cock," Anton says laughing. A sparkle flickers in his eyes, then he jumps from his seat and runs inside, knocking the bottles of vodka over on the table, some smash onto the floor. Kazier manages to save two of them and shakes his head.

"Look," Anton says holding out a long-ass surgical needle. Everyones eyes go to him, all eyes wondering what the fuck he's talking about. Then he pulls his shirt over his head and pinches one of his nipples between his fingers, he looks around, his eyes landing on me last.

"You... you're fucked up the most. Pierce this shit," he says nodding toward his nipples.

Maybe I've had too much to drink. Maybe I want to hurt him. Either way, I stand up and take the needle from his hand. He grabs one of the bottles of vodka that wasn't smashed, takes a long drink of it then pours it over his nipple, then nods his head once to me. He's about to say something when I grab hold of his nipple. I watch his mouth open then just before he says a word, I stab the needle straight through. His eyes go wide, then he screams. Very loudly.

I step back, leaving the needle through his nipple then grab the bottle of vodka he had and pour it over. He screams again, this time pulling a hunting knife from his pocket and swinging it at me. It cuts my face, just barely, and I take a step further back.

"Next one," Viktor says holding up his bottle in salute. "This is the best night. You screamed like a bitch." Viktor's mouth twitches in amusement.

"It hurts, you son of a bitch. Let me do you now, fucker." He reaches down and pulls out another needle, waving it in Viktor's face.

"Do I look like a dickhead to you? You hold onto that title perfectly."

Anton's eyes go to mine, then he points the needle at me. "You, you big ape, take your fucking shirt off."

I shrug my shoulders and do it. He smiles while holding the needle. He pinches my nipple, a tad bit too hard then I feel the slice as it punctures. When I look down the needle is hanging right through.

"Fuck off! That stings like a bitch," Anton says looking to my nipple then to his. He grabs the last needle and holds my other nipple.

"Look at you two love birds, grabbing each other's nipples and shit. Bonding. Aww…" Kazier laughs.

"Your next, fuckhead," Anton says then stabs the needle straight through my other nipple. He looks pissed when I don't scream. I actually didn't even feel that one. Maybe it has to do with the alcohol that I know as sure as shit, is coursing through my veins right now.

"So, you both plan to have needles as your piercings? Did you even think this through?" Viktor asks looking at both of us one at a time.

I look to Anton. It was, after all, his smart idea. One that I stupidly went along with.

"Didn't think that far ahead," he says sitting back down.

Kazier starts laughing hard, and Viktor joins in. Anton shrugs his shoulders and hands me the vodka. We both sit there topless, with needles in our nipples. Maybe it's a new trend—a very stupid one at that.

CHAPTER 12

Pollie

After Death had dropped me off, I felt empty, that there was something missing. I've never felt that way, and it made me think my feelings for him are growing stronger by each second. I didn't expect to have such strong feelings for a man that can't possess them. I'm not stupid and naïve. I know he's a bad man, I know he does terrible things. I know he's as cold as the ice in the Atlantic, I even know he tried to kill me. Though he somehow stopped himself from slicing my throat before Elina shot him. I shouldn't have gone anywhere near him after that night, but I can feel he's fighting something I know nothing about. I feel his tension each time I'm within his distance.

He doesn't tell me much, and what he does tell me is hard to decipher. I ended up going to work for practice after he left. With having nothing to do, and staying with him all night, I needed to work him out of my mind.

When I arrive home Elina is on my doorstep, her arms wrap around me. I can't return the favor as my hands are full—my violin in one hand, my cane in the other.

"I'm having a small hen's night, and I want you to come. You're my best friend Pollie, and the only person I want there with me. The only problem is Kazier demanded I take Freya as well... they're waiting at the local bar for us."

With a nod of my head, she follows me inside my home and soon after I can hear her ruffling through my closet. She walks to me and places clothes in my hands.

"Wear this. It's girls' night, and you're going to look fabulous."

"What is it?" I ask because I have no idea what she's pulled out.

"It's just a skirt and shirt to show some boobies. You have beautiful tits," she says cupping my breasts and pushing them up. I shoo her hand away and remove my clothes and begin to dress in the clothes she gave me. When I feel the length of the skirt, I gasp. This skirt was given as a gift from Elina ages ago. I never intended to wear it once I knew the length of it. Trust her to be the one to find it stashed in the back of the closet.

"This is too short, Elina. I can't wear this," I say shaking my head. No way, I'm pretty sure if I bend over you'll see everything.

"Yes you can, and you will. My night. My choice. I choose what you wear."

I walk over to her and touch her hips, they're bare. Her shirt sits just under her breasts, and her skirt is probably shorter than mine. I pull my hands away.

"Are we hookers for the night? Is this a dress up evening?" I ask clearly confused.

She laughs at me. "Hunny, this is how I always dress."

A part of me doesn't want to believe that she does, though I have a feeling she's not lying one bit. She sits me on the bed and starts playing with my hair, drawing it up and pulling parts out.

"You have the most beautiful colored hair, Pollie. It's blonde, but it looks like you have streaks of brown through it. It's gorgeous."

I thank her, even though I've never seen color and have no real idea what she means. And when she's finished, she doesn't waste any time placing a glass of champagne in my hand.

"Hold on... don't you hate Freya?" I ask, remembering she's coming too.

"Yes, well... no. Not really."

"Okay... that makes perfect sense," I say with a laugh.

She pulls me by the hand telling me our ride is here, and the whole walk out to the car my hands are on my skirt trying to pull it down, just so I don't flash anyone.

****

"It's not as loud as I thought it would be," I say as we enter the bar. Elina has hold of my hand as she guides us to a table.

"I wanted to have a night with you. So I prefer it to be not too loud, that way we can talk."

I nod my head in understanding. Sometimes I feel like a burden, and I realize the real reason she's not going to a club is because we can hardly talk, as I won't be able to hear her speak over the loud music. Then I remember it's not because of my disability, she'd go to a club if that's where she wanted to be. I try to not let my disability affect my life as much as possible. I try to take control, live as normally as possible.

Some days are harder than others, but some are easier. With Death, they're the easiest. I don't know why yet, I can't comprehend my feelings. I just know his emotions are strong and that I never have to second guess him. I always know where he is, always know what he wants. In some way or other, I can tell if he wants my touch, and for some reason it calms him. The only thing I still don't know is the way he feels toward me. That's an issue I haven't yet conquered.

"They're here already?" I'm confused for a second. "Who else?" I ask.

She leans in close when she speaks. "Some friends of hers. She didn't want to come by herself, I guess." I feel the tension as soon as we reach the table. It's like a cloud of smoke building up around us.

"Freya, thanks for coming. This is Pollie," Elina says, grabbing my arm and pulling me down to sit. Freya says hello and introduces her friend as Angelina.

A waiter walks up and Elina places an order. No one is speaking to anyone, it's all extremely awkward.

"Aren't you the girl that was with Death that night at the club? He took you out over his shoulder, right?"

I can feel all eyes are on me, I know they're waiting for my answer.

"Is he the one with the dark hair and deadly face?" That must be Angelina.

I hear Freya answer, "Yes."

"Shit, that man is mighty fine... and scary. Imagine him in the bedroom."

Everyone laughs. I don't. I know what he's like in the bedroom, and I hope they never find out. *He is mine.*

"Pollie, what's going on with you and Death?" I just hear Elina's voice, she's whispering so no one but me can hear her. I shake my head, virtually telling her I will talk to her later. I don't want her to tell her here.

Elina changes the subject. I silently thank her, and soon everyone is chatting, and actually behaving. I don't know much of the story between Freya and Elina, all I do know is that Freya was arranged to marry to Kazier, which never happened.

"I miss him. Want to come back to mine?" Elina

asks with enthusiasm in her voice.

"You just want sex. We don't need to see that or be around for that," Freya speaks.

"No. Come on... I have champagne. Plus, I know there's always vodka stashed around the house."

The word 'vodka' seems to do the trick with everyone agreeing.

****

Climbing up the stairs we hear voices, I pause, and Elina tugs me up.

"You didn't say anyone else would be here," I murmur as she continues to step up.

"Of course, the boys stayed here for their night."

"Figures..." I hear Freya mutter from behind me.

I finish stepping up and then walk through the door. Loud male laughter fills the room. Then it goes silent as we wander in, and I realize they know we're here. I hear kissing, and I know straight away it's Elina and Kazier.

Then I hear Freya's friend whisper to Freya. "He's here. Do you think he's single?"

And my body tenses at her words. I don't wait to hear her response as I walk out to where the boys are quietly talking. I try to not think about that night and this place when I step outside, and the cold air hits my skin—my very bare skin. I reach for a chair and feel someone push one behind my knees. I smile and sit down, hearing Freya and Angelina wandering out as well. I don't know exactly who's here, but they're friends of Kazier's and Elina's, so I feel somewhat more comfortable sitting out here.

"Freya…" Anton addresses her.

"What."

"Don't steal my vodka, bitch."

She goes to say something but then all of a sudden she's laughing. Hysterically.

"What the fuck have you two done to your nipples?" she manages to push out in-between her now hysterical laughter.

"We pierced them, right Death?"

My body goes rigid, those words are directed right near me. I should have felt him, but I didn't.

"Are either of you planning to remove the needle? Or just keep it stuck in there like that?"

"We didn't think that far ahead," Anton says confused.

I hear Angelina speak when she says, "Hi," to someone, and I guess that someone is Death. He doesn't respond to her, at least I don't hear his response. Then she pushes it further. "Want to come and grab a drink with me?"

I stand then and turn back toward the door. Not wanting to hear anymore, I walk to the bench, my hands come into contact with its cool top.

"Why are you wearing that?"

My spine straightens up, I turn to his voice from behind me. He steps closer, and I can smell the alcohol on his breath. He reeks of it. I don't answer, and he reaches out and runs a finger over the top of my bare thigh. "Why. Are. You. Wearing. This?" he asks again, pausing at every word. My hand comes up and I touch his chest. I feel something cold and sharp and pull my fingers away remembering he's pierced his nipples. That means he's sitting out there shirtless, and Angelina is probably ogling him. I feel jealousy course through me.

"Why are you shirtless? Shouldn't you at least have a shirt on in front of other people?" I snap too harshly, and my hand flies up to cover my mouth, not understanding where that venom came from.

He presses himself to me, I feel the edges of his stomach, his muscles touching me. He keeps one hand on my bare thigh.

"What was that for? It couldn't have possibly been from jealousy, right? Not sweet little Pollie..."

I hide my smirk in his chest. He knows. And he's toying with me. Playful? Dare I call it that? How much has he had to drink?

"Death, we haven't finished you bastard. Hurry the fuck up."

He grabs hold of my hand and pulls me as we walk out the back. I feel for a seat, when he grabs my hips and pulls me onto his lap. His hand comes back to my thigh, then it creeps into the middle, blocking any view anyone would have. His mouth comes down on my shoulder, he bites it softly and I moan ever so slightly. Thinking everything is right, just for now.

CHAPTER 13

Death

I can actually stand to be around him, and I actually find him funny. Maybe it's the alcohol because I feel the need to kill him subside and wash away. Watching Pollie walk in, and sit right near me, almost made me lose my cool. Her skirt is too short, her breasts are too exposed. I feel the need to cover her up and touch her.

She got jealous. I didn't think she had a jealous bone in her body, but I was proved wrong. Freya's friend makes her jealous. I like it. No, I like it a lot.

My hand creeps in between her legs, she sighs into me, leaning back with all her weight. I take it, not caring if she moves the needles still sticking through my nipples. I turn to the side, Freya's friend is watching me with beady eyes. Her eyes are on my hand that's between Pollie's legs. She catches me looking and smirks, but I turn away. Not wanting a thing to do with her. If she was a hooker, maybe. If she was Pollie, definitely.

Kazier sits across from us, his hand wrapped around Elina's chair, touching her back. She smiles up at him every time she speaks, then gives her attention back to whoever is talking. They plan to marry in secret, everyone knows they will marry, but they don't want anyone to know apart from us. Too many enemies. Anything to bring him down a notch and kill those he loves. His main weakness is her, and she's a prime target for our enemies. No matter how skilled she is, she can't out-power twenty men. Her eyes look over at me, she looks to Pollie who's sitting on my lap, she then looks back at me. Her lips form a thin line, and she stands moving over and touching Pollie's arm. She leans down, whispers something and Pollie shakes her head. Then she steps back to where she was, picks up her drink takes a sip then starts staring at us again.

"What was that?" I ask into her neck.

Her shoulder curls up from my breath on her neck, and she whispers, "She wants to know what we are."

"And what are we?" I ask because I don't even know.

"I don't know, I still have to work that out."

That answer disturbs me, I don't know why. Is it because I want her to tell everyone she's mine? Or because I don't even understand what it is I want?

"I have to go home," she says while standing. Her ass comes into full view of my face, she leans over just a tad to grab her cane and my cock stands tall. When I stand, I almost knock her forward. My cock pushing into her, I manage to catch her before she falls and bring her back to me.

"We're out," I say holding onto her hips.

"Fuck off, soft cock, you can't go yet. We need to do something about those tits of yours," Anton says pointing to my pierced nipples with a bottle of vodka in his hand. He can drink, I think he's drunk more than all of us here combined, and he still seems soberish. How that is possible, I don't know.

"Tomorrow," I say pushing Pollie to walk. She doesn't disobey and says goodbye to everyone but doesn't stop as we walk from the house. "You're coming to mine," I tell her while calling a Uber. She looks down, her hands wrapped around her waist and nods her head. I don't touch her, just watch. Her blonde hair is up, showcasing her face, her legs are sexy as fuck and begged to be cut, just to have some sort of imperfection. Her breasts, well, I can almost see all of them. Her creamy skin look delicious, and I want to do bad things to it.

Together, we don't match. Me with tats covering my face and body—rough, scary, are a few of the words used to describe me—her, well, it's absolute beauty. And it scares the shit out of me that I'll change it, change her, when that's the last thing I want to do. Not one thing is wrong with her. Not her caring nature, not her sweet voice, not her hands that play her instrument like it's her life source.

Not one single thing.

The car shows up and I don't touch her. My head is slightly clearing now, the alcohol wearing off. She sits with her legs crossed and doesn't speak on the drive. I don't speak either. The car comes to a stop, and she pulls the handle climbing out and stays standing on the side of the road as she waits for me.

"What's wrong?" she asks once the driver leaves, and I stand where I am staring at her. I know she can feel it because she fidgets with her skirt. "If you don't want to talk, I can leave."

My heart hammers one large beat, and I step up and take her face, bringing her in hard so my lips smash to hers. She immediately opens her mouth and kisses me back. I pick her up, her legs wrapping around my waist as I carry her up the stairs all the while kissing her and never removing my mouth from hers.

I slam her back into the door, wondering if she'll bruise. She pushes her chest into mine and digs her nails into my back.

"Inside," she says just as my hand snakes in-between her legs. She pulls her mouth away and lays her forehead on mine. "Why do you want me? Is it just for sex?"

I unlock the door and carry her inside, she doesn't speak waiting patiently for my answer as I walk her up the stairs.

"Don't ask me questions I don't know the answers to."

She drops her legs from clinging around my waist. "I don't know you. How am I meant to get to know you?"

I pull away from her and remove all my clothing. "Get naked!"

She drops her head.

"I'll answer one question for every item of clothing you remove," I tell her knowing she doesn't have much on. She stands and places her hands on her hips and pauses for a moment, her face a mask of disbelief, then proceeds to pull her skirt down and lets it drop to the floor. Underneath is only a thin piece of fabric, and I know if she turned around all I would see is her ass.

"Love, I want your thoughts on it."

"It's not real. It's what people tell one another to make them feel better. It's all in the brain, some sort of chemical reaction. It's not in the soul."

Her eyebrows scrunch in confusion. "Really, you don't believe in it at all?"

"That was two questions. You only removed one piece of clothing. You want the answer... lose the top."

"That wasn't a question."

"So you don't want the answer?"

She waits a moment then pulls her top over her head. Breasts spring free, no bra.

"No, I don't believe in it. It's fake. The word is overused. It's not real."

She goes to speak then shuts her mouth very quickly. She only has one piece of clothing left, if you could call it that.

"Last question… make it count because I will."

She takes a deep breath as I wait for her next question. "What do you do *exactly* for work?"

I knew she'd want to know sooner rather than later. Now I have to decide if I water down the version of what I do, or if I tell her straight. I have a feeling she couldn't handle the full extent of what I do. She pulls the final piece of clothing off, standing there like a goddess who's about to be eaten by the devil. Pity she doesn't know it yet.

"I work on the dead." She pales, her mouth forms a thin line. "Now that your question is answered…" I say stepping toward her. Her hand reaches up, and she touches one of the needles then she pulls away.

"You like pain?" she asks, but I think more to herself than to me.

"Yes," I reply, not even knowing if she expected an actual answer in return.

She reaches up and starts undoing her earrings, then holds them out to me. "Put these in. I don't want to touch them."

I take them from her hand, and she stands there waiting for me to do as she wants. Pulling the first needle free, I replace it with her earring. It slides in easily, then I do the same with the second, placing the needles on the bedside table.

A knock comes hard on the door, just as I place my hand to her hip. I want to ignore it when it comes again even louder than the last time. She turns her head toward the sound and then my name is called. Not my name now, my birth name. And I know exactly who it is.

"What's your name?" she asks shocked. She can feel me tightening up each time that name is called. "Tell me, tell me your name … not Death. I want to know. I think I should know this!"

"Dmitry."

"Who downstairs knows that name?"

"My brother," I tell her through clenched teeth.

Pulling away from her, I start stepping down the stairs.

CHAPTER 14

Death

His hand is paused ready to assault my door again when I pull it open. He's dressed in all black and stands at the same height as I do. It's been months since I've spoken to him, years since I have seen him. He looks me up and down and pushes past me to enter my house. He takes a long look around then comes back to stand in front of me.

"Clothes?" he asks, his eyes full.

I shrug my shoulders. I didn't intrude into his house late at night that was his doing.

"You've been ignoring me, Dmitry." He hears soft footsteps upstairs, and he looks to the staircase. "Do you have a hooker up there?" he asks pointing in the direction where the sound just came from.

"No."

He shakes his head and takes the steps two at

a time as runs up them. I'm inching behind him and manage to grab his shirt, pulling him back and slamming him into the wall just before he opens it. He gasps loudly.

"What are you doing?"

I hang my head, then look at him with confliction.

He can't go in there.

He can't see her.

I don't want him near her.

The door opens, and Pollie's head becomes visible. She stands there dressed.

"You do have a hooker…"

My palm digs into his throat, cutting his air off. That's the last thing she is. To say that makes my blood boil. Pollie's hand touches my shoulder, and I loosen my grip on his neck but keep it locked just in case.

"I'm going to go," her small voice speaks.

My body falls just slightly in disappointment. Sebastian turns his head to look at her, properly look at her, then his eyes swing back to mine.

"You like her?" he teases. He can see the

reaction I have for her. Pollie's head swings to his voice then she grabs her bag from the floor and touches the walls as she walks closer to me. I watch her hand and demand it doesn't touch him, she lifts it when it comes closer and touches my waist giving me a gentle squeeze as she continues to walk out. I stay where I am, Sebastian glued to the wall and now watching the empty stairwell.

"Never thought I would see the day..." he says as soon as the door closes.

I push free of him and walk straight into my room, slamming the door and pulling on my pants. This wasn't the plan I had for the evening. The plans didn't involve him at all—they involve Pollie and only Pollie, marking me, and me fucking her until I passed out. Which has now gone to shit.

When I pull the door open, Sebastian is standing there with his hand rubbing his neck. He drops it and stands in front of me.

"We need to talk, and you *will* talk since you made me come in fucking person," he says as he turns and steps down the stairs. I stand there watching his retreating form. He has on black slacks, a black button down shirt—our dress styles don't match. He is class, I am not.

"Why are you here, Sebastian?"

I take the seat opposite him. He gazes around my empty apartment. Nothing personal is in this space, just a couch and television.

"You left the house?" he asks surprised.

I never told him I moved. That house has been sitting there for years with no one going into it.

That house—it's the root of all evil.

"You grow some brains while you were gone? Obviously, you can see that..." I roll my eyes at him. "How did you find me?" I ask since I never told him where I live.

"Kazier's father."

I nod my head. He would tell, Kazier wouldn't.

"You're working closely with Kazier now? One of his three, I heard?"

He left solely based on that. Not wanting to be that close to everything, he hated the killing, but he liked the after part. Something we have in common, though the killings don't bother me as much as they bothered him. I nod my head.

"He didn't marry the daughter?" he asks sitting back.

That could be why he's here. He works directly for Freya's father, and Kazier's father promised him that Freya would be married to Kazier. That didn't happen.

"Is that why you're here?"

He blinks a few times, and I know the next answer he's about to give me is a lie. It's his tell. He should know I know this.

"No, I came to proposition you."

He could be telling me the truth, though I doubt that's the whole truth. He's bulkier than I remember, not as large as me, though. But he definitely has more substance to him than when he left. He looks more like our father, whereas I took after our mother. Olive skin, dark hair, dark eyes to his lighter complexion, his lighter hair.

"Tell me so I can go to bed." I lean back in my seat, and look down, Pollie's earrings still in my nipples. I wonder if she made it home. I wonder if I can make it there with her still awake so I can fuck her. My cock twitches at that thought.

"He wants you to work for him, he has a great opportunity."

I start to shake my head, then he throws the money figure at me. I've never cared for money, I was raised with it. I've seen greed and what it does to people. I hardly cash my checks now that I receive. I live off next to nothing, I have enough money in my bank to last me a lifetime and then some.

I stand and walk to the door, his eyes follow me. I pull it open, waving a hand out. "Get the fuck out."

He stands, stretching his legs and walks over to me. He leans in and looks me in the eyes.

"I've heard stories about what you've become, brother. I hope it's not true. Once you go down that black hole, there's no escaping. Look at Padre for example..." he trails off when he notices the anger brewing on my face.

I don't reply. Instead, I say, "Get out."

He looks at me as he passes raising his eyebrow, and I slam the door harder than necessary when he leaves. He's lucky he is my brother, or his body would be on my table downstairs right now, being cut open while he screams.

CHAPTER 15

Pollie

I don't want to be involved in family business, so I got dressed and left as fast as I could. Now I'm standing just down the street from Dmitry's house. It feels weird to know his name, it suits him much better than 'Death.' Death has such finality. The word means to die, to end, to expire. I hate it. He's more than that, a lot more. He's not death to me, rather life, energy, vitality.

His brother called me a hooker. I don't know how I feel about that. So I shake it off and try to focus on something else. Like why I almost slept with him, again. I don't do these things. Normally, I know someone well before it gets to that point. Dmitry and I are not at that point. Actually, we are far from that point—I know very little about him.

"What a sight," a voice comes from behind me. I jump, and my hand goes to my chest. I can feel him close. He's quiet, much like his brother, though I can usually always feel Dmitry. "You love him?" His hand comes up and brushes my hair away from my face, lingering a second too long for my comfort and I pull away.

"I don't think... I should be going," I say turning back to the road, hoping the taxi arrives sooner rather than later.

"I can see the appeal. Your skin is like nothing else I've seen or felt."

That comment sends shivers through my body. I don't know what he means by that. I know Dmitry loves my skin as well, he's always touching it. But to hear it from his brother as well, I don't quite understand.

"He's intrigued by you, I can see why."

I don't hear his steps they're so silent, but I hear when his voice changes direction and comes to stand back in front of me. He waves his hand in front of my face, I can feel the air movement when he does. I reach up to knock it away.

"You're blind, right?" he asks himself more than me.

"Yes," I tell him, hoping my answer doesn't give him an insight into my disability so he can use it against me.

"So you don't know what he looks like? How evil he really is? How he looks at you?" His laugh is vile, then his voice is close, I can feel his breath on my lips. "He looks at you like a canvas. He isn't sure if he wants to paint you, or keep you plain."

My eyebrows scrunch up into a scowl. What on earth does that mean? What is with all the cryptic messages?

"What do you mean?" I ask voicing my concern. I'm sure he can hear the tremble in it.

"You know what he does, right?"

I nod my head. "He works on the dead."

"Yes... Yes, though my boy is a bit more twisted than most. You see... his view of death is more like an art. He takes great joy in tearing that body apart, burning every bit of it, 'til nothing is left but acid. You see, he learned it all from me. All except for the last part. I burn my bodies, cremate them if you will. Dmitry, well, he takes a lot more care. He has fun with them."

My hands begin to shake, I can feel my breathing pick up.

No. He couldn't do that. No way.

"No," I say more to myself, but he hears my response.

"Yes! And I would be careful if you don't want to wreck your canvas. Because I'm pretty sure he would love too..." He doesn't say another word just withdraws, leaving those words dangling there. Leaving me standing on the side of the street, scared and worried.

****

I stay in my apartment for two days. I miss work, nor do I answer my phone when it rings. I remain in bed, the only time I leave is when I have to eat or use the bathroom. I don't know how to feel about any of it. A part of me is screaming to run away, to never see him again. He could kill me at any minute, at any second. And I wouldn't be able to stop him if he did. Then there's the part that says if he hasn't already, why would he now? I mean he tried, and he didn't finish, though. So why should I be worried, I shouldn't. Then I slap myself and tell myself not to be so stupid, one slip with a knife, just one moment, and he could take my life while I lay next to him asleep. And I wouldn't be able to defend myself against him. He would overpower me in an instant.

After three nights a knock comes on my door,

it's loud and hard, and I know it's him. He's the only one that would come this late and wake everyone up. I hear him say my name, but I don't move, instead pulling the covers up over my head in the hopes he'll go away.

He comes again on the second night, later than last night, and wakes me from my sleep. He stays longer, knocks harder, I'm almost afraid he'll break my door down.

Then on the third night, he makes me squeal. I cover my mouth with my pillow so he doesn't hear me. He stays longer and longer each night, his voice beckoning me to come to him, to let him in. I don't, I still don't understand him, let alone understand what we are to each other. If we even are anything, and I won't put my life at risk like that.

The fourth night comes, and he doesn't knock as hard, and he doesn't scream my name. It's a softer knock, more a plea for my name. I fall asleep listening to him saying my name over and over again.

I leave before he's due to arrive on the following night. Knowing I'm caving, that soon I won't be able to resist and will pull that door open. So I head to the studio for work, I haven't practiced in almost a week. When I arrive only the director of music is there. I hear him shuffling papers. I walk past him and straight for the practice room to set myself up. A little later he comes in to check on me, his footsteps stop at the door. He doesn't speak, just listens to me play and then walks away.

On my way home, I feel lighter, more at one with myself. Being able to play, is like an outlet, an outlet I never knew I needed until the day I picked up a violin. I didn't think I would be able to play, in my condition, but that wasn't true. I worked hard to learn as much as possible, to be able to play at the level of people my age, then I soon became better than them. And before I knew it, I was being hired straight out of high school with the many job offers that came my way. I never planned on my love of classical music to actually become my occupation. To me, it was more of a passion, something I truly enjoyed doing. But the moment the opportunity arose, I knew it was what I wanted to do and what was needed in my life.

My phone rings as soon as I enter my building, I don't answer it. Feeling better, and more refreshed, I choose to ignore anything that might put a damper on my mood.

So I lie in bed, and fall asleep, without the knocks from Dmitry which I secretly miss.

****

Nights come and go, and I wait each night for his knocking. I stay up later than I normally would, each day telling myself I may let him in, but he never comes. A few nights later, earlier than he typically comes, a knock sounds and I race to the door. Upon pulling it open, the smell that greets me is a disappointment. It's Elina. Not that I don't want to see her, I was just hoping for it to be him, to maybe get some answers now that I've had time to cool off.

"Well, don't look too excited," she sneers as she pushes past me. I stand with the door open for a little longer than necessary then close it and follow her inside. "I can't stay long, but I have a present and some news…" I hear the ruffling of fabric and the noise of a zipper, "…I bought you a dress," she says excitedly.

"What for?"

"For my wedding, of course. You're Maid of Honor."

My mouth drops open. "When's the wedding?" I knew she was getting married, but I didn't know when and that it would be soon.

"Tomorrow." She claps her hands then places

the dress into mine. I feel the silk under my fingertips, its feels beautiful and elegant.

"What color is it?" I ask running my hand over so I can feel it—it's a long cocktail dress. Even though I have no idea about colors and what they look like, I want to make conversation. I've been told that colors can be brighter or sombre and it helps to know if I'll be dressed in something light or dark.

"Baby Pink." She leans in and kisses my cheek. "Make-up and hair will be here tomorrow. See you then," she says bouncing out the door, she stops just before it closes. "And I haven't forgotten you avoiding my question about Death. I *will* want answers after the wedding." She walks out and the door slams behind her.

I step across to the door, lock it, and carry the dress to my room laying it out on the chair in front of my bed. He will be there tomorrow, I'm sure of it.

I guess tomorrow is better than never to talk to him.

CHAPTER 16

Death

She doesn't answer. For nights on end, she doesn't answer. I don't know why. It couldn't have been what I do, I told her, and she was still ready for me to touch her. She doesn't fear my touch. So I can't figure out why she won't see me, especially when I know she heard me.

I do the same thing she does, only stepping out of my home to knock on her door late at night. I stay in my basement, ignoring the bangs on my door, the screams from others.

I work and work. And do nothing but deface and destroy the bodies that are sent my way night after night. I requested more, they don't argue, then the next night I'm delivered two bodies. I didn't go to her that night. I stayed where I was, doing what I know will never disappoint me or fuck me over. I cut, tear, and burn each and every limb. Sometimes I go to the extreme of removing eyes when I'm truly lost. I want to keep them, place them in a glass jar and store them on a shelf. But I know I'm not allowed to. All evidence must be destroyed, no matter the circumstances. We can't risk being found.

When I come up, the sun has risen, and the light hurts my eyes. I don't look around when I enter, but a voice stops me from stepping forward.

"You think you can hide?" Kazier's voice booms from behind me. How long has he been here for? Waiting for me. He looks pissed. A lot of people don't scare me—actually, none do. Though I know he could kill me without a second thought, and make it worse than I could possibly imagine. I have, after all, dealt with all his kills for most of my life. "I've been knocking on your fucking door for three nights, Death. Three. Fucking. Nights. Did you know your scum of a brother was back in town?" I nod my head and stay where I am, he looks up to me with a sharp look. "You didn't think to inform me of this?"

"Why?"

"I could kill you right now for being so fucking stupid. I swear to God." He starts cursing in Russian, flapping his hands around everywhere. "I'm getting married tomorrow. Bring your fucking brother so I know where he is at all times," he says walking to the door. He stops when he opens it and turns back to me. "You better fucking be there. If you're not, don't expect my next visit to be a friendly one." He slams the door on his way out.

I step the rest of my way up the stairs. Stripping off my clothes to rid that smell of death, I turn on the water as hot as possible, scorching my skin. Pain, pain is what I need right now.

****

Sebastian comes when I call, I didn't even need to tell him to dress up for the occasion. He already is, I knew he would. He comes dressed much the same as he was that night, this time he has on a red tie and it matches the color of fresh blood. He walks in and looks me up and down. I have on a suit, the only one I own. It's for the family, our family crest sits on my cufflinks. He eyes them too.

"We going out?" he asks.

Grabbing the keys to my car, I nod my head. He doesn't question and follows me out, my hair is slicked back. The length of my Mohawk has grown, I haven't had it cut, just the undercut redone. He pats my head and laughs as he climbs into the car. His hair is perfect, not a single hair out of place. That's too much energy for me, to be that perfect.

"Kazier's wedding. Best behavior," I tell him.

He nods his head in understanding, though he doesn't say anything else. I wonder why that is, why there aren't any questions.

When I pull up to the park where the wedding is being held, I spot Anton, Viktor, and Kazier straight away, all dressed in black. All looking sharp as fuck.

"Not many people, you sure I was invited?" he asks looking at the men who have spotted us. Anton gives me the finger, and the other two just stare.

"I was instructed to bring you," I say pulling the handle.

His arm comes over to my shoulder. "I don't think we should go."

I squint my eyes at him. "You don't have a choice, get the fuck out." He doesn't leave the car straight away, Sebastian sits there and I ignore him and walk straight to the boys. Sliding my sunglasses over my head, Kazier nods and rubs his hands together. The only people here are us and the celebrant that will marry them. He looks nervous, though, his eyes keep on moving to Kazier then back to the ground. I suppose he should know who he is.

"He plan to get out of the car?" Viktor asks nodding his head toward Sebastian. I look back and see him still sitting in the car, just staring out at us. He notices us watching and climbs from the car.

"Here comes the dickhead now."

"Don't start, Anton," Kazier says warning Anton. He puffs out a breath and turns around, his back now to Sebastian. Sebastian shakes Kazier's hand and drops his head in acknowledgment, then steps back to stand next to me.

"He send you?" Kazier asks Sebastian, speaking about Freya's father.

"He did… for Dmitry."

Kazier's eyes go wide. "His name is Death, and you can't have him," Kazier says straightening his spine.

Sebastian keeps his mouth shut. He knows not to argue with Kazier, he is, after all, our boss, and he's not in Russia anymore.

A car pulls up next to where I parked. We all turn and watch as the door opens, a heel steps out, and I immediately know it's Pollie. Her soft skin calls my name. She stands tall and turns offering her hand into the car. Her dress clings to every section of her perfect body. Her small curves look like the dress is made of a second skin.

Elina steps out, dressed in white, a black sash wraps around her waist, and curves up her back like lace. I turn to look at Kazier, his eyes bright as he watches her.

Love, that's what he calls it. I see it in his eyes. I wonder how long that will last. Love never does, it's all in their brain. Just a chemical reaction that likes to fuck with us.

"Can I hit that?" Anton nudges me nodding toward the girls. I know he isn't talking about Elina, he wouldn't dare. He's talking about Pollie, whose arm is wrapped in Elina's.

"Can I kill you?" I retort not looking at him. He laughs softly then he shuts up when they get closer. Kazier takes hold of Elina's hand, leans in to kiss her on the lips, but she stops him with a finger to his lips.

"After," she murmurs.

He shakes his head and stands tall. "I think this is my favorite, and I can't wait to tear it off you," he says eyeing her dress. She smirks and turns toward the celebrant. I twist to look at Pollie, her hands are joined together holding the flower bouquet. Her head is down, and she doesn't move as the words begin. I don't even hear the words. All I'm thinking about is taking her away, and possibly keeping her locked up so she can't make me go through this again.

I take a step closer, her head lifts, and her spine straightens. She knows it's me. Sebastian is watching us, I can feel his eyes on me, but I don't care.

"Pollie," I whisper, her head turns toward me then back again.

"Shhh…" she whispers paying attention to what's going on. I turn my head back and my hand comes up to touch her, it slides along her back which is covered in silk, and I stop just above her ass. She takes a deep breath. "Someone's here," she whispers.

I don't know what she means at first. Of course, there's people here. Then I turn to look around and a man is walking toward us, eyes covered by dark glasses and something black in his hand.

"Kazier…" My voice isn't raised as I'm trying to gain his attention. The minute he turns to face me he gives me a deathly look and then he sees it and his body covers Elina's by stepping in front of her. A single shot rings out, and we watch in fascination as it flies past us and hits Kazier, knocking him and Elina to the ground.

I grab Pollie's hand and thrust her into Sebastian. "Take her... *now.*" He looks back, then grabs hold of her hand pulling the keys from me and runs with her to the car. Viktor has his gun raised, Anton is running toward the man with his gun extended in front of him. He doesn't stop when a bullet rings out, he doesn't even move out of the way. Viktor fires a shot, I watch as it shoots straight past Anton and lands in the man's leg. It doesn't stop him, he just limps then straightens up.

Other men come up from behind him. Anton pauses running, coming to a halt, and pulls his own gun. I go straight to Kazier. His eyes are closed, and Elina begins screaming, blood soaking through her white dress staining it red. She doesn't move him, just clings to him.

She looks up when I reach down for him, reaches into his pants, pulls Kazier's gun just as I lift him up. She stands, tears running down her face, covered in blood and turns her stare to the men. She walks fast, raises the gun and aims it. Shooting the first shot. It's perfect. An absolutely perfectly shot and the first man drops to the ground.

"Don't kill them," Viktor shouts.

Her death stare turns to him, and his head drops. Anton has tackled the second man with the gun, and he has him pinned to the ground. She walks straight up to him, pushes Anton with her free hand, he moves but keeps his foot on the man's shoulder. Then without so much as a blink, she shoots him in the head.

She drops the gun, turns back to me, tears still in her eyes and walks toward me. If she weren't about to get married, I would take her and keep her. That's some serious shit. And she looks like the bride from hell, which amuses the crap out of me. I don't wait for her to reach me, I start to run to his car, passing the celebrant on the ground who's dead.

"Clean-up," I yell, knowing Viktor will call someone to deal with it. I throw his body into the back of the truck. Anton comes out of nowhere and jumps in next to him, and I take him to the family doctor, speeding like it's my own life on the line.

****

Anton carries him straight in, the doctor is already set up, gloves on, and starts tearing at his clothes. Kazier's heart stops as we place him on the table, so the doctor begins CPR, and when that doesn't work he brings the paddles out.

The door opens and Elina rushes in, she runs straight to him and touches his face after a pulse finally rings out through the monitor. She sighs in relief. The doctor immediately starts working on getting the bullet out. I walk away and let her hold his hand as the doctor works on him.

Viktor pulls up just as I walk out the door. "Your house," he says telling me the bodies are on their way. I leave planning to get lost in death.

CHAPTER 17

Pollie

I heard footsteps but didn't think much of it. Elina told me it was a secluded park and that the only people who knew about the wedding would be there. So when I heard the footsteps, I had to say something to make sure it wasn't someone uninvited. I never thought it would be followed by gunfire. Though with this family, I shouldn't have guessed anything less.

Death was touching my back, I didn't tell him to remove his hand, I've missed his touch, the warmth of it. He pushed me into someone else's arms, I didn't know who that person was until we reached the car. Sebastian told me to buckle up and sped out of there. He asked me where I lived, but I told him I wanted to go to Dmitry's, and he didn't reply.

When we finally stopped, he touched my arm

and told me to wait. We sat in the car for a few seconds longer then he asked me, "You sure this is where you want to be?"

I just nodded my head and climbed out. I don't know why it's here I need to be. I just know it's where I came last time I was scared, last time I heard gunfire.

He unlocked the door for me but didn't follow me in. I shut the door after me and was expecting Sebastian to come in with me. I waited on his couch for over an hour until the front door finally opened.

"Dmitry?" I asked. It was more than the sound of one person's footsteps. They stopped at my voice, and I heard something drop to the ground. They didn't answer me and they walked out. I stepped over to where I heard the thump, my foot hitting something hard on the floor. I dropped to my knees and felt for it, coming into contact with clothes, then blood, then skin. I scampered backward, landing on my ass.

"Pollie," Dmitry's voice calls for me.

I don't get up, my body is in shock, fastened to the floor. My mind is baffled, but all I see is bad. A body is on his floor, and he doesn't seem to care. He touches my arm, and I pull away scurrying backward.

"Don't touch me," I squeak out.

"Pollie, you know this is what I do."

I shake my head at him slowly. "You're sick, aren't you? Just sick," I spit out.

"I'm me, Pollie. Nothing will change that."

"This is why you don't do relationships, right? Too many secrets, too much death." My hand covers my mouth, I now understand his name completely.

"No, it's by choice. I don't like anyone."

I scoff at him and manage to pull myself up. Walking around the other side to where his voice is located and around the body, I fall straight down over another body. My hand comes in contact with more dead skin. I scream and struggle to get up, I'm sitting in a room full of dead bodies. Me living, and Death just surviving, for God only knows why.

"What's wrong with you?" I scream at up at him.

His hands come under my arms, and he pulls me into his chest he then moves me away from the bodies. When he puts me down his hands skim over my sides, and continue further down until I push them away.

"Why have you been ignoring me?" he asks.

I shake my head not believing he doesn't care that three dead bodies lay on his floor. He would rather talk to me about why I haven't spoken to him in a week.

"Your brother told me what you do. How you burn…" I can't finish that sentence.

"Sebastian is filling your head to scare you."

"Are you telling me he's lying? That these bodies won't go with you to wherever it is that you go, and you won't cut them up and burn them in acid?"

He curses in Russian. I recognize those words from Kazier.

"Yes. I told you what I do. How do you think I got my name? You think I sew them back together and give them back with pretty fucking little bows in their hair?"

I throw my hands up in the air, I don't want to be here anymore. "Go and fuck one of your hookers," I scream at him turning to find the door.

"I prefer to fuck you, my little porcelain doll," he screams at me.

I run, not caring that I don't know where I'm

going. Bumping into walls and God knows what until I find the door. I push my way through and race away.

I shouldn't have done it, I shouldn't have gotten so worked up because I don't hear the car that pulls out in front of me, the one that knocks me to the ground.

****

I wake with the smell of Dmitry all around me. I try to move and my head thumps when I do. I touch the back of my head and feel dried blood. I can feel the sting on my elbows and notice that bandages seem to cover them.

"You're awake…" His voice comes from next to me, but he isn't in the bed. The mattress is empty with just me on it.

"How long…" I ask touching my head again.

"Not long. You've woken up twice, and gone straight back to sleep. The doctor checked in on you a few times."

"I should go…" I try to sit again and groan when my head pounds.

"I have to wake you every three hours, you hit your head hard. Why the fuck didn't you hear it,

150

Pollie? Tell me why you ran straight into a fucking car. Are you trying to punish me?" I go to speak, then he continues, "Congratulations, you did punish me. I haven't fucking moved. I've never worried about someone so much in my life. My fucking heart was beating out of my chest as I saw the car approaching. You didn't even hear me."

I don't even know what to say to that, though I do know I want to leave. I absolutely don't want to be here right now—near him. Especially knowing that three dead bodies are downstairs.

I go to sit up, my head feels woozy. My hand lands on my chest, and it isn't silk that covers my body anymore it's a shirt, and it's his. His smell is all over it. I go to stand and feel my legs begin to wobble. So I sit back down.

"What are you doing?" he asks me, now closer than before.

"I'm leaving. I am *not* staying here with you… with those bodies." I shake my head at the thought.

"You can't leave."

"I can," I argue back standing up. I manage to stand longer this time, without falling.

"If you want to go home, I'm coming." I hear him walk past me, then hear the sound of drawers opening and closing. He walks back to me and his arms come under my legs, he picks me up like a lover would carry someone they adore. I try to not melt into him. It's hard, though, having him so close. He walks me down the stairs, then carries me to his car.

I don't ask him if he's coming inside when the car comes to a stop. He gets out and picks me up before my feet even touch the ground. I don't argue with him, I really just don't want to. I hate confrontation, and I feel we've reached our maximum for the day. He has the keys before I even think about where they are, and he opens my door, walking me in and placing me on the bed. He tucks me in, then I feel him slide in next to me.

"What are you doing?" I ask. His hand comes down and latches onto mine.

"Sleeping, I haven't slept for over twenty-four hours."

I let it go. And before I know it, I'm asleep, passed out with my hand linked in his.

Like nothing has happened.

Like my floor wasn't ripped out from under me.

Why do I let him continue to do so?

CHAPTER 18

Death aka Dmitry

She's still asleep when I wake, her hand still pressed into mine. I remove it, and she turns onto her side. My shirt she's wearing skirts upward revealing her ass. I have to control myself not to touch her. Throwing on my clothes, I take one last look before I leave, grabbing her keys on the way out. I didn't sleep long. I wanted to sleep longer with her, except the bodies are calling me. The itch I feel that three bodies are sitting in my basement right now is greater than ever.

She doesn't want me around, I can feel it. I just haven't accepted that fact yet. I don't know if I ever will. If she doesn't, I plan to keep her, with or without her acceptance. Then there's Sebastian, who I know is to blame for it all. For the way Pollie sees me, to the reason Kazier is unconscious right now. All him.

He came for me he says, but I don't believe

that's the only truth. He wouldn't have come all that way just for me. Sebastian doesn't even like being here because he's told me so before. He prefers Russia, he prefers his new boss.

So for him to come here just for me, is not believable. And if he's as close as I think he is too his Parkhan, he would do just about anything to please him. Even killing family.

I expect him to be at mine when I arrive in the early hours of the morning. He isn't. I don't even know where he's staying. He could be staying at our family home, the one I haven't been back to for years and never intend going back to.

My hand hovers over the security door for the basement, when I turn around he's closing the front door. Pulling open the door that leads to the basement, I step down and hear his soft footsteps as he follows me. I pick up my saw and ignore him. He leans against the wall, the red light shining on his face as he watches me with fascination.

One of the bodies I drained while Pollie was asleep. I grab it and carry it to the table, the others have their own tables, but are not prepped to be cut. All their clothes still on, all belongings still in their possession. This one I stripped, and he lays naked on the table. It was the celebrant, the one with the worried eyes. He didn't have much on him, only his book and a set of keys. The other two I know for sure will have weapons. I look up to Sebastian then back to the two bodies of the guys that ruined Elina's day. Wondering if he's really here to see me, or to hide what I may discover.

His eyes bore into mine, I don't talk to him and begin to carve away at the first arm. The music is loud, it's programmed to turn on when the door opens, or I personally change it myself. I expect him to have a retort to do with the music. He preferred classical while he worked, I prefer heavy and intense, something to help me with what I do. Bad matching bad.

The first cut is always the biggest rush, it's what pushes me to continue with the rest. The bones are always the toughest. Sometimes my hands will be red and sore for days with the amount of pressure I need to apply to get through the bone. I have a chest full of saws, I go through them continuously. They don't hold their sharpness once you cut through multiple bones.

My gloves go on—and I forget Sebastian is even there—then the mask and apron. He's watching now with intense eyes. I realize he hasn't actually seen what I do. Yes, he taught me almost everything I know about bodies, just not the logistics of pulling one apart. That I learned all by myself.

Each part of the body I remove from the man enters the barrel of acid. It sizzles when it penetrates the surface. I watch him take a step closer, just not close enough that it will affect him. His hand lifts his shirt, and he covers his mouth with it to stop the smell. It's not very pleasant.

Once all body pieces are in the barrel, I place a lid over it, then I walk to the other bodies, feeling my hands in their pockets. I look up to Sebastian when my hand touches something. I pull out a cell phone, place it next to me and keep on feeling around. Then I pull out a knife, the same one as the other man has in his pocket. I look up to Sebastian with his eyes glued to the cell.

"Anything you want to tell me?" I ask him, he looks to where the body is in acid, then back to me.

"You love it, don't you?" he asks surprised. "I thought it was just something you had to do, but you love it, don't you?"

"I don't love anything."

His head drops to the side assessing me. "You do, and it's not the only thing you love. She is, also," he says referring to Pollie.

"You don't know what you're talking about." I grab both cell phones and pocket them, then remove the gloves, mask, and apron.

He starts to walk up the stairs ahead of me as I follow heading straight to the front door, looks down to my pocket and holds out his hand.

"Give them to me," he says nodding toward the cell phones.

"Kill me first."

His hand drops and he looks to the floor. "You choose them over me? They would kill you in a heartbeat, Dmitry." His eyes pin mine.

If I did something wrong, I have no doubt that they would kill me in a heartbeat just as he said. But I'm not the guilty party here, he is. And he knows it. He pulls a gun from his shorts, aims it at me, I stand and wait. I don't even know this man in front of me, not anymore.

Did I ever really know him?

He was the only person in my life for years, but now he isn't.

"The only way you're getting these phones is to pry them from my fingers, Sebastian."

He holds the gun steady, then he slowly lowers it down. He shakes his head and puts the gun away.

"You want me dead, just like our father?"

I don't know how to answer that. I don't, but if he brought it upon himself, I can't help that either.

"You dug your own grave the moment you came home to fuck with the family. You of all people should know how they operate. You lived it longer than me, saw it first-hand."

He looks out the door, his shoulders tensing, then back to me. "She won't love you. I'm the only person left on this earth that will love you. I hope you take more care of my body when you get rid the evidence."

"That was also your fault. What did you say to her exactly, to make her so scared of me now?"

His lip twitches. "You shouldn't be interested in someone like her. I set you up with the hookers for a reason. I have something dark in me, but it shines more brightly in you." He doesn't look back as he walks out slamming the door as he goes.

Stepping down the stairs, with both phones in hand, the sun is now rising. Pollie will be awake soon, and I need to get back there before she wakes. I slide the screen on the first phone and go to the calls. The same international number was dialed twice in one day. I press the phone to my ear listening to it ring.

"Hello," is heard from the end of the line in Russian. It's a man's voice. One I don't recognize. I know Freya's father's voice, and this is not his. I do the same with the next cell phone, the same man answers in Russian.

What has he gotten himself into?

****

I left the other bodies where they were, not wanting to miss going back to sleep next to her. When I unlock her door, no sounds are heard. I walk to her room and see her in the same position she was in when I left, curled on her side her ass visible. If she weren't sore right now, I would take her, and make her mine. But she is, and it's partially my fault.

My phone vibrates as I start to remove my clothing. I look up to make sure it didn't wake her. I wonder if she knows how stunningly beautiful she is, if she has any idea what she does to the male population. It isn't fair to compare her to anyone else. Where some woman scream sex, Pollie screams comfort and beauty. Unlike most women I've encountered.

"He's awake," Viktor's voice booms through the phone.

"I'll be there in a few hours." I don't wait for a reply as I end the call and climb into bed next to her, my fingers graze her ass, soft as silk. She must bathe in lotion every night to get her skin like that. She moans just slightly turning to her back. I grab her hand in mine and she clasps it firmly in her sleep.

And that's how I fall asleep with her hand stuck in mine. Trying to figure out what she means to me.

What is she to me?

How come I can't walk away or fuck her like I do my hookers?

CHAPTER 19

Pollie

I wake with a hand wrapped around my waist, a heavy hand at that. I can feel his breath on my back, he's asleep. I push it away slowly and manage to sit up on the bed. My head spins, and I realize I need to eat something, I haven't eaten since yesterday morning before the wedding. Just as I stand his breathing becomes uneven and I know he's awake. I pause at the door, waiting for him to confirm it, but he doesn't.

"Leave Dmitry," I say with my back to him. I hear the bed creak as he gets off, and he comes in close proximity with my back. He presses his body into mine, and I know what he wants straight away. I shake my head and pull open the door walking out. He doesn't follow, and I listen as he starts moving around. I pull the fridge open and grab out a packet of strawberries to eat. He walks in, his scent is right near me, clogging my brain with my need for him.

"Is that what you want?" he asks me. I nod my head placing a strawberry into my mouth to stop any words to the contrary. He steps closer, his breath on my ear, "The only reason I'm not taking you right now is because you're sore, and not in the way I intended for you to be." He nips at my ear before he walks past me and straight out the door. As soon as I hear the door close, I drop to the floor. Not sure what I've gotten my heart into. How come I was so blinded by everything that I didn't see the danger that lay ahead? I'm not invisible, I'm just a girl who stupidly fell for an undertaker.

****

I don't have any family, I hardly have friends. Elina is what I consider to be my best friend. I have people who I talk to at my work, but they're colleagues. My boss, I speak to more than anyone else there. He's always polite with me, always showing and teaching me ways to improve. When I walk in, I know it's just him there for the day. He basically lives at the school. On top of it being a school, it's where we rehearse after hours for our next performance. Sam says a brief hello to me as I walk past his office. I sit down in my regular seat and start to pull my violin out when I hear Sam's footsteps come in. I look up to his direction so he knows I can hear him.

"You look upset," he says.

My eyes go back to the ground, back to pulling my bow from the case.

"I'm fine," I reply curtly.

"You've been coming in a lot more at night time, Pollie. Something isn't right, tell me?"

I shake my head, he doesn't need to hear about what's wrong in my life. I wouldn't even know how to describe it, where to begin or how to tell it.

"Just drama."

His arm snatches my elbow as he turns to inspect it, and I pull it back and slide my jacket back on.

"What happened, Pollie?"

"I ran into a car, clumsy, I know," I say half laughing, hoping he'll drop it.

"You are the least clumsy person I know, and that's saying something since I work with stiffs all day," he says jokingly. Sam is only a few years older than me, I don't know what he looks like, but his voice is kind, and he's always nice to me. So I have nothing but respect for him.

"How about we go and grab something to eat? Put the violin away, you can practice whenever you want. You don't need to practice." My hand holds the violin, and I'm gripping it hard, he's never offered to see me outside of work before. Always here, never anywhere else.

"Just something to eat?" I ask wanting to confirm that, that's all this is.

"Yes," he replies as he walks off and comes back with a set of keys. I've already packed up my case and am standing waiting.

****

Sam's good company, he doesn't ask anything too personal, he keeps it all light and to do with work which I find refreshing. The last thing I want to do is answer questions, or be investigated about anything, especially regarding Dmitry. He knows I've been seeing someone, I told him when it first happened. Though I didn't think much of it when I said it, it was the first night Dmitry, and I had slept together. I assumed it meant more, it obviously didn't.

Just as he's halfway through a story about one student, he stops talking altogether. "Pollie, a man is standing behind you," he whispers the last part, knowing only I will it hear it. "And he looks very dangerous."

My spine straightens, and I instantly know it's not Dmitry, his smell and his presence aren't invading me. It's someone else. A hand touches my shoulder softly, and I try not to jump from my chair.

"Pollie..."

It's Sebastian, I know that voice, he's the one that cracked open my façade and made me see the truth of who Dmitry really is—the undertaker. Well, that's how I like to refer to him.

I smile at Sam. "You can go, Sam. I promise I'll try to pop in tomorrow to see you." I hear his chair scrape as he stands.

"Are you sure? I can stay." I hear in his voice that he doesn't want to be here, he wants to go and is thankful for the out I'm giving him. Except, he wants to make sure I am okay. He's a good man. I nod my head, and his hand touches mine on the table, and he squeezes just before he leaves.

Sebastian walks around and takes the seat that's now vacant. I hear the sound of the chair pulling out as he sits down. My hands play with the food in front of me, not having an appetite anymore.

"Boyfriend?" he asks quizzing me.

"Why would that be any of your business?" I ask him.

"It's not."

"Glad we've got that covered. Now can you tell me why you're here? Are you following me?"

"You weren't hard to find." He doesn't give me much, and it makes me angry.

"Again, why are you here?"

"He loves you, did you know that?"

My heart pumps hard in my chest. My face goes red. I can feel it heating up.

Is what he says true?

It can't be, Dmitry doesn't do love, he's told me this.

"He doesn't do love."

"Touché, he doesn't, but whatever he wants to call it. I'm sure it's all to do with you."

I stand, his arm touches my hand.

"I know my brother, and trust me, you're his new obsession. That should scare you."

I sit back down pulling my arm away from his grasp.

"Why would that scare me?"

"Do you want to end up on the same tables that he uses? Do you want him to tear you apart just so he can see your insides?" I shake my head, of course I don't. "Has he played with your blood?"

My head rears backward. What?

"I don't understand."

"He likes hookers. I used to buy him hookers. One hooker was his favorite as she liked to dabble in blood play... during sex."

"He has never hurt me, after that one night," I say remembering the first time he almost did with his knife to my neck.

"He will, soon your skin will harden, the appeal will be lost. So what's left of you once the obsession of you dies down? Can you really trust him one-hundred percent?"

"I'm not seeing him anymore," I reply standing and this time walking away.

He does follow and offers to drive me home. I don't decline because I already fucked the devil. What's another going to do to me?

CHAPTER 20

Death aka Dmitry

Kazier was moved to his home when he was unconscious, the doctor staying there to keep an eye on him. He's awake I've been told, so as soon as I leave Pollie's, I make my way over to his house. Bag still packed and horny as fuck.

I need to fuck a hooker. That thought makes my cock instantly soft.

What has she done to me?

The door is unlocked when I enter, the house is quiet. I find both Viktor and Anton asleep, one on the floor and one on the couch. When I make my way to his bedroom, Kazier is looking at Elina, her body is half on and half off the bed, and she's sound asleep. Her dress still bears the blood of Kazier. He doesn't move much, his hand glued to hers. He sees me enter, and points to her, indicating I pick her up and move her to the bed. I grab her from under the legs, her dress is thin, and it sticks to her as I lift her up. I expect her to move, or protest, something, but she doesn't make a sound.

"She's only just gone to sleep," Kazier's voice comes through hoarsely answering my unanswered question. I place her next to him on the bed, and she stays in a ball. He brushes her hair away and kisses her cheek before he attempts to stand. I immediately come to his side, but he brushes me away as he comes to a full stand. As he goes to take a step, he almost falls. He shakes his head, and I don't give him a choice as I hoist my arm under his and help him walk out of his bedroom. We step to the couch that Anton is currently asleep on, I kick him hard, and he jumps ready to attack. When he notices it's us he calms down and moves out of the way, kicking Viktor awake as he goes past him.

"Did you find anything out?" he asks.

Both men are now standing, all eyes are on me. I pull the cell phones from my pocket and give them to him. He grabs them scrunching his eyebrows as he looks over each one. He does the same thing I did, straight to the recent calls and presses call and places it on speaker phone.

The voice that answers the phone this time is different from the first. This time, a shiver runs up and down my spine as the person answers in Russian. Kazier's eyes shoot to mine, he knows that voice as well as I do. He hangs up before he says anything, passing the cells to Anton to search more. He's useful for something, he is a king with gadgets.

"That wasn't who answered when I called earlier," I tell him. His eyes are evaluating me to see if I'm lying. He nods his head and just as he's about to speak, the door bursts open and yelling commences. Anton groans loudly.

"Why have you been ignoring me? Why hasn't anyone answered my calls?" Freya screams.

Viktor walks to her, places his hand on her back to calm her down. She flings his hand away and places her hands on her hips. Then she walks around the couch, Kazier sits down gingerly with bandages wrapped around his waist and shoulder.

She rolls her eyes at him. "You're sore, so you ignore me?"

"He just woke up, woman, from almost being dead." She turns on Anton and slaps him hard across the face, he laughs it off as she turns back to Kazier.

"What happened?"

"I tried to get married."

Her eyes go large with shock. She apparently didn't know. She looks around and sees the guys still wearing their suits they had on. Obviously, they haven't left his side. Unlike me.

"Is she alive?" she half-whispers, unsure if she should ask that question. "And why the fuck wasn't I invited, I was meant to be the bride."

"Yes, she's alive, but she's asleep."

She nods her head and sits down.

Kazier looks to me then back to Freya. "Do you know a man by the name of Boris?"

She thinks for a second, and her eyes go wide as she looks at me.

"You look like him," she says.

I try to not hurt her for that comment. She must see it in my eyes because she backs away.

"I only met him once, maybe twice. I came here when I was a teenager, remember. But he always scared me." She looks back to Kazier. "Why?"

"A hit was put out on me, or Elina, I don't know which."

"How would they know where you were?" she asks the question everyone hasn't asked. Kazier looks to me.

"Sebastian," I say quietly.

"It's his Padre, he's always had a hold on him."

"He's meant to be dead," I announce. He was shot to death, I was told this, Sebastian told me this fact.

"Liars," Anton hisses shaking his head. Just as we're about to speak, a voice screams through the walls then a woman appears, in a once white dress, looking very pissed.

"Get back to bed. *Right. Fucking. Now,*" Elina screams the last part.

Kazier goes to stand, and I help him again. He turns to Elina and smirks at her.

"If you shower, I will stay in that bed with you and never leave."

She looks down and snickers. "I wanted to be the Bride of Chucky." She laughs but it's fake. "Tell them all to leave." She waves her hand and turns her back to us.

"We aren't leaving you. Someone needs to be here to protect you," Anton says.

As soon as those words leave his mouth, a gun fires, everyone ducks but Kazier. He laughs, and it's real.

"Unless you want a bullet in your asses, leave this fucking house," Elina says holding a gun in her hand.

Anton swears in Russian, hoping she doesn't understand. But she aims again, and his arms fly up as he makes his way to the door. The rest follow him while I have a hold on Kazier. Freya is the last to leave, she drops the gun and walks off. We hear the shower start, and as I walk him back to his room, he asks me something.

"Send Pollie over tomorrow, she needs someone."

I nod my head and walk him to his room not saying anything more as I leave. We know what's about to happen, words aren't needed.

As soon as I close the front door behind me, Anton is sitting on the steps outside. He turns to look at me, flicking his smoke to the ground. "He's dead you know." His eyes hold mine, waiting for a reaction. I don't give him one, and walk straight past him. "I need a fuck, come to this club with me, they won't let me in by myself anymore."

I stop and think about it. Could I find a hooker that looks like Pollie and fuck her? "Why not?" I ask him.

He shrugs his shoulders. "Some shit about I can't control myself…" He laughs it off as he climbs into my car. I guess I'm driving then.

He talks about pussy the whole drive, about how many times he will fuck tonight. I don't give him any encouragement. He has a whole conversation with me without myself uttering a single word. He pulls his jacket from his body, places his hand on his cock, gives it a shake and wears the biggest smirk as we walk into the club. It's packed, bodies everywhere, men near the stage, women walking around naked. Anton walks straight to the private booth throwing money at the man in front of it and makes his way in.

I follow him in and watch as he picks up a woman and listen to her fake giggle that follows. She acts like she enjoys it, it's a lie.

A woman comes to me, she starts dancing when I sit, her ass in my lap, then in my face. Trying everything to get me to touch her so she can earn the money that her friend is about to receive from Anton. When I turn to look at him, the girl is bent over on her knees. He kneads her tits in his hands, all the while she bobs up and down sucking on his cock.

"You want the same?" the girl asks me.

I shake my head, I don't want my cock sucked, I want to cut. And I know this woman isn't someone that would allow me to do that. I run my hand along her skin, closing my eyes hoping I can pretend for her to be Pollie. I snatch my hand away, she's not. She isn't as soft, her skin isn't as pure. I can feel bumps on it, there's no perfection there. Nothing like Pollie's. I stand pushing her ass away from me.

"Where are you going?" Anton calls out as he pushes the girl's head down further onto his cock.

"I'm out." And I don't look back as I drive home, wondering how I could get Pollie to suck my cock.

CHAPTER 21

Pollie

The day after my encounter with Sebastian has me a bit torn up regarding his words about Dmitry. I need to stay away from him, as far as possible. I can't let him get under my skin, I'm not cut from the same cloth as him.

I like flowers and life. He likes death and more death.

Not one thing about us matches, complete opposites in every way that's possible. I try to look beyond that, but I just can't get the feel of those bodies from under my hands, the same ones I know will be on his. I shake the thought from my head, and when I open my front door to walk out, I run straight into a hard body, that's not recognizable at all. Strong hands steady me as I back away.

"It's me," Sebastian says removing his hands. I back further into the house, and he follows me inside not closing the door.

"Why are you here?" I didn't think about it when I took a ride from him that he'd end up on my doorstep the following day. Before he can answer me, I'm pushed backward, my ass lands straight onto the floor. I hear the grunt of a male I recognize. Then the smash of something against the wall. I listen to the sound of a fist smash against skin, then I bend over and scream, scream so loudly that the only thing I'm able to register is the sound of me.

Hands pick me up from the floor, pull me into their chest. I know who it is. I push away, trying to distance myself from him, from all of this.

How is this my life now?

"Calm down." His voice is soft, I don't recognize it at first because his voice is anything but soft. I start smacking him, my fist connecting with anything they touch. He doesn't stop me until my last punch is done. He just stands there and takes it. "Calm now?" he asks still standing in front of me. I feel his body turn then his voice goes hard again. "Leave, right now."

Sebastian does as he says. I hear his footsteps as he walks away. Then the door shuts when he's gone. I step away from him, not wanting him to touch me.

"Leave," I ask of him, just as he previously asked his brother.

He takes a step back from me. "Pollie…"

There it is again, that soft voice. Where is that coming from?

"Leave…" I say again.

"Just let me say what I came to say," he asks me.

I nod my head.

"I don't know what you're doing to me. I don't understand it."

"Is that all?" I know my voice sounds distant, not attached.

"Elina needs you."

I nod my head, and he doesn't say another word as he walks out the door. I drop back to the floor, curl myself into a ball and cry. For reasons I don't understand, though, my chest hurts, a lot. And I can't seem to make it stop.

****

My eyes squint when I walked outside, I managed to pull myself together enough to make my way to Elina's. When I knock, no one answers the door. I knock harder and the door swings open. Elina's smell greets me, and she pulls me in tight for a hug. I can feel her breathing heavily. I wonder if she just finished crying too, if today was the day that our hearts have had enough and decided that it was time to let some of our distress out.

"Thank you," she says pulling back and dragging me into the house. She takes me in a different direction than I usually go. I hear ruffling on a bed then Kazier greets me, my mouth forms a smile, but it's forced. He thanks me for coming, which is very unlike him, then Elina asks how I've been. I don't want to burden her with anything so I simply shrug my shoulders. I hear the sound of kissing, then she's pulling me back out and into the main area of the house. Sitting me on the couch, with her next to me.

"Spill, take my mind off it all." I shake my head at her. "Spill Pollie, tell me what it is with you and Death. Don't deny it."

"I don't even know. It was good, so good. Then it was just…"

"He told you what he does, I take it?" I nod my head. "He's very… unique, I guess you could say."

"Or evil," I say shrugging my shoulders.

"Yes, but I have seen him with you. I don't think he is when you're with him."

"He did try to slice my throat open, remember?" I reply sarcastically.

"If he wanted you dead, Pollie, not even Kazier could stop him."

"That doesn't make me feel any better."

"I'm just saying how I see it. I don't know him, I've only heard about him. And not one thing has been pleasant. Though with you, he's protective, and I actually believe he doesn't even know what it is that's affecting him. Maybe you need to make him see it."

I let her words sink in. I do believe with me he's different, if there's a difference. I don't know the real him. Only what I feel, and hear.

"I don't know if I want to do that anymore. It's all so tiring, and I'm not sure if I can get past any of that..." I trail off, and a shiver breaks over me thinking about those dead bodies I touched. I hate it. Yet, it's something he's used to doing.

"Well, at least tell me the sex is good?" She laughs.

I hang my head. "It's the best. I've never, you

know… never had someone so… into me."

"I've slept with a lot of people, ain't no denying that. But I knew something was different when his hands were on me. Even if I fought it for as long as possible," she says referring to Kazier.

"Sex can't be everything," I groan laying into the couch.

"But what a great way to start." She laughs. "Got to make sure he knows how to use it."

"I touched one," I say my head falling down, I don't know if it will ever leave me.

"He isn't killing them, Pollie. He is simply doing what he gets paid to do. He may love it, but maybe you don't understand why he does. Have you asked? Have you tried to be near him when he does what he does? Maybe get a feel for it all?"

"No way… no way…" I panic.

"If you like him as much as you're trying to deny it right now. Why not at least try?"

"What if he gets over me… you know, in the future? What if I become just another thing in his life?"

"I doubt that, but when that time comes, you'll know what to do. You just have to ask yourself is he worth it? Is your heart worth it? Because I'm telling you now, love is better than running away from it. If I had to choose life or love, it would be love every time. Without a doubt. He fills me up like no one has ever done before. Don't you want that?"

I nod my head. I do. I so badly want that.

"Go! Go home and think. All I can tell you is that it's always worth it in the end."

"I'm sure you weren't thinking that the other day."

Her hand comes to lay on top of mine. "If he died that day, I wouldn't regret a single thing. Every milestone put me in a path for him, it was my walking stones."

"What about your family? Have you heard from them?"

"Only Maso, that's all I need... Kazier, you, and Maso. I don't need anyone else. You three fulfill me enough." I stand and lean in to cuddle her. "Now go. I need to see if I can ride my not yet husband's cock without hurting him." She laughs following me to the door.

CHAPTER 22

Death aka Dmitry

The pain was there, I caused it. How did I cause it? I don't even know. The break in her voice, as she asked me to leave. I didn't understand it. Women don't cry around me, they usually run. I've never dealt with such things. Ever. And Sebastian, I don't even know why he was there, how he even knew where she lived.

I don't trust him, not around her. He would see her, I know he isn't blind. She's unique. She hardly sees the bad, until it's forced upon her, like the bodies.

Was that her turning point? Touching them, the lifeless corpses that were mine for me to do my work. I didn't know. A part of me was screaming not to care. How did I come to care, even in the slightest for her feelings? I have no idea.

The sex was great. Her body, her skin, were

mine. I wanted to claim every inch of her. Like it was my last breath. I intended to. I've started to put a plan together, to kidnap her, lock her away for only me to see. She could be my little doll, to do with as I please. Maybe so I could search her, insides as well as out for what she has and how she has a hold on me.

Then somewhere in my fucked up brain, I knew it wasn't the way to go with her. I would never see her again if she managed to escape. She wouldn't have that strong grip she has on me when I take her, she wouldn't bite me until I bleed if I did that. And I needed that pain she would inflict in the heat of the moment.

My car comes to a stop out the front of a house I never want to go into ever again. One I said I would never enter again. But I need him gone, or dead. I haven't decided which yet.

The gates open, and I know he's in there when I drive up to the front of the house. The door is open, and no one stands there. My hands squeeze the steering wheel, willing it to pull around and drive away. I don't want to go back in there. I hate it.

The house is exactly as I remember it when I left. It's big, old, and magnificent. My father used to tell us never to touch anything. That our mother decorated this house and if we destroyed something, we would get a belting. It was like living in a museum, that was my mother. Her frames still hang on the walls, her beautiful smile, that I wondered if it was ever forced, stares back at me.

How could someone so good, love someone so evil?

He was, evil. I have no doubt about him in my mind. Not once did he care for us, not once did he tell us he loved us. It made us both who we are today. Cold-hearted bastards I guess, just like him.

I hear a voice in the foyer, my boots drag on the white tiled flooring as I enter. Sebastian is there, a glass in his hand, smiling at me. He places his cell in his pocket, holds up his drink then places it to his lips.

"You haven't been back have you?" His fingers brush along a table, picking up dust that has accumulated from years of neglect. "I went downstairs. You didn't take any of my tools, not one. Or anything from your room. Did you hate this house that much?"

I scoff at him. He did as well, but for a reason. It wasn't only so that he wasn't under Kazier's father. He hated it here as much as me.

"Why were you there?"

My fists clench into my hands, I release them, then clench them again. Digging them deeply into my skin, so my nails break the skin. Blood.

He walks around the dusty table, his finger dragging along it wiping off the dust then he turns to me. "I can see why you're fascinated with her... quite lovely isn't she. She may be blind, but she sees things we don't, doesn't she?" He looks at me then checks for my reaction. "You may say you don't love. But I have news for you, you love her, so fucking much. I can see it in your eyes with the mere thought of me mentioning her name."

I take a deep breath and attempt to calm myself, trying hard to not pull the gun out that's in my back pocket and aim it at his head. To kill him.

"Why. Where. You. There," I ask again.

"I like her..." is all he gives me.

I shake my head like I didn't hear those words and scrunch my eyebrows, just trying to make sense of everything.

"She's scared of you. Did you know that? Have you been inside of her yet? I bet it'd be heaven." He whistles that last part.

Three giant steps and I have him by his neck, holding him up. His hand clings to mine, striving with his fingers in an attempt for me to release him. Then a slice is made with his other hand on my arm. Blood starts to slide slowly then drop to the floor, and I release him.

"I know about your blood play," he says coughing, my head swings to his. "You don't think I didn't fuck that hooker as well? That I didn't know what she was doing up there with you in that room?" He points up the stairs to my old room. "I was the one paying her, Dmitry."

I had no idea he knew. I didn't think she told anyone. The only people who knew were those I'd fucked, or so I thought.

"They *will* be coming for you, and I won't stop them," I say stepping back from him.

He laughs, but it's hollow. "Do you not know... by now, who sent me?"

I do know but choose to ignore that fact.

"He's been working for Parkhan ever since he covered up his own death. He wants Kazier dead just so he can come home. Take the reins."

"It won't happen."

"But it could. Tell me, what's the easiest way to get to him? Would it be by killing his men?" I don't answer him, it wouldn't be. "Or would it be by that sweet piece of ass he has with him all the time?" My brother's lips twitches, he knows he's right.

"I won't kill you today, I won't give you that satisfaction. I *will* let him do it. But remember, at the end of the day, it's your body that will be in my basement." I turn to leave when his voice follows me behind me.

"What about when it's his? It is him you really want, isn't it? I am just a pawn he has used all his life. Think yourself lucky, Dmitry, that you could get away," he says referring to our Padre.

I don't wait to hear anything else as I leave that house, I don't want to hear any more. He may be a tool in the game, but it's a dangerous game he's playing. He's on the wrong side. And for that, he will end up where they all end up, in my basement.

****

When I arrive home, both bodies have been drained. I remove one, pulling the body down from the hook and placing it on the table. I grab my saw. Music blares, blocking out the noises in my head as I start to chip, break, and tear away body pieces like a jigsaw puzzle. Just as I remove the first arm, a shoe appears in my doorway at the bottom of my steps. Then I watch as that person comes into view. No one would be crazy enough to come down here, let alone come down here with the knowledge of what happens. If it were a threat, they would end up only one way, the same way everybody ends up who enters, in a barrel full of acid.

"Fuck!" Anton screams as he looks at the last body I have drained. I turn to see what he's swearing at. Nothing is out of the ordinary. The body has cuts all over it, dark red stains the skin from the dried blood, a clear mat and buckets are underneath hanging by the hooks. Less clean-up for me.

Shaking his head, he grabs a mask holding it up to his face as he walks over. He leans over to the man who now has one arm removed and his eyebrows rise. "Can I have a go?"

I shrug my shoulders and pass him the saw. Watching as he passes through the skin easily, then when he reaches the bone, he doesn't get far as he struggles.

He shakes his head, passing it back to me. "That's crazy man."

It is, and it's fucking hard work. An electric one would save me so much time, but I don't care about time. Me and time aren't friends.

"What?" I ask looking up as he watches me finish what he started. The trick is to use all your body weight, as much as possible to hack through the bones.

"Viktor has your brother…" My eyebrows scrunch, I was talking to him.

"He followed you," he says answering my question. "Well, we both did." He smiles like he's proud of it.

"And?"

A simple shrug is all he gives me before saying, "Just thought you should know, in case you wanted to say goodbye."

Do I? I don't even know. I don't seem to know much anymore. I preferred my previous life, before her. Send me the fuck back in time, before Pollie, before I had to leave this house to become one of Kazier's four trusted men.

"Where is he?"

Anton smirks. "At mine," he answers walking up the stairs, leaving me here with the bodies, my only constant.

CHAPTER 23

Pollie

I'm wallowing, is that a word? I don't even know. I can't stop thinking about what Elina said. Should I? Or shouldn't I? A part of me wants to follow my heart and stuff everything else, then my head comes into play. Raging thoughts about how bad it is and that I shouldn't be associated with that, or even be near that, ripple through my brain. My life was happy, flowers and rainbows and all that shit. Then came a spark, a spark I didn't know about when he touched my hands, holding them like I'm his lifeline. That spark is still there, I don't know if it will ever go away. I just don't know what to expect from him. What I should expect? He has saved and protected me on every given occasion, never thinking twice, but then there's the fact that he also tried to end me. I feel, no I know, I'm safe with him around, without a doubt.

It's been two days since I kicked him and

Sebastian from my house, I haven't heard from him at all. I sometimes wake up in the middle of the night, thinking he will be back, knocking on my door, or beside me. Neither has happened. I decide today is not a day to dwell, so I head to the shops, intending to buy myself something, anything, in an attempt to make myself feel better. I ring Elina to join me with no answer.

When I arrive at the shopping center, I sit down on a bench. I like to listen to everyone, to their conversations. Some people like to people watch, I like to listen. If you listen closely, people let a lot of things slip when they think no one is listening. I feel someone take a seat next to me, which is not unusual; I've probably been sitting in the same spot longer than thirty minutes.

"Interesting aren't they?" the voice speaks.

A shiver runs down my spine. Whoever this person is, I don't feel comfortable, nor safe. I nod my head not making conversation, but being polite. I'm never rude or mean. I don't like the effect it has on me. Pulling someone up is so much better than bringing them down.

"I'm Boris," he says.

I turn to the direction and smile. "Hi," I say turning around, away from him. I grab my cane and open it. As I stand, I can feel him watching me. I don't look back as I walk away.

I decide that my plan didn't work, no boost was given. I think it's time I sat down with him and talked. Otherwise, it's just going to continue to eat at me.

Making my way outside, I wait for a taxi. As one pulls up, I open the back door and recite my address. Just as we pull away, I know something is wrong. I can feel it like it's eating away at my core. I need to get out, now.

"Fancy running into you again." The voice jumps from right next to me. I reach for the door handle, but it doesn't move.

I'm not even in a taxi—the inside is leather, this is a luxury car.

How did I miss that?

How did I not feel that when I got in?

My mind is too occupied, my usual senses not kicking in.

"You didn't tell me your name?" he asks again, this time closer. I hear him take a deep breath as he breathes me in. "I can certainly see the fascination with you." My head swings to him. "Ahh... you're slowly putting it together, aren't you? You know why you're here, right?" I shake my head. "I need him to do something for me. But he doesn't listen to orders unless they come from one person... Kazier. I believe he *will* listen when he hears your voice, though."

"I wouldn't count on it," I say backing up to the door, away from him. I hear his phone pressing numbers, then he places it to my ear. Then I feel something cold pressed to my stomach—a gun.

"What," Dmitry's voice sounds through the phone. He sounds... broken, in a way. The gun presses harder into my side.

"Dmitry..." my voice squeaks.

"Pollie?" he asks shocked.

"Yes. Yes, it's me."

"Why are you calling me from an unknown number, Pollie. Where are you?"

I squeeze my eyes shut tight. "This man said you have something or someone he wants." I hear him swear.

"I'm coming, Pollie, I'll find you," he says just as the phone is lifted away from my ear.

The man next to me speaks into the phone. His

voice calm, and collected. "My boy, lovely to speak to you..." he pauses, and I can't hear Dmitry's response. But I hear the man's chuckle. "You see, they have him. If you want her... alive that is, or possibly untouched, you'll bring Sebastian to me. But Dmitry, if I see anyone else but you, I have a bullet just for her." I hear him end the call then relax back into the seat.

"Who are you?" I ask.

"I'm Boris, love, I don't lie."

"Yes, but why me?"

"He doesn't care for anything or anyone. He would kill his own brother if he had to. And not blink twice. I didn't expect that from him. He was, after all, my youngest son. He didn't speak much growing up. Then I heard of you. What a pretty little toy you are to him." His fingers brush through my hair.

"You're his father?" I gasp.

"Yes, and I came back to take what's mine," he says just as something covers my mouth. I fight against it, but his grip is too strong.

****

I wake to feel my legs and arms strapped

together, and it hurts. Cold tiles sit beneath me. I attempt to break out of the bindings, by pulling on them when I hear his laugh close by.

"It's quite convenient you being blind and all. You don't have to see him for what he really is." I hear the pouring of a liquid, then drinking.

"And what is he?" I argue back. Not being able to move.

"He was nothing growing up. His brother was hardly anything either. But I could see the potential there. A few years ago I started to hear stories. I thought nothing of it. They were about a man named Death. Quite fitting really... that name, considering his job..." he pauses, and something comes to my lips. He holds the glass and my mouth is assaulted with vodka, removing it once I have no choice but to drink. "So where was I, that's right... Death. By this time, I'd been gone for a few years, never once thought about Dmitry at all. He reminds me too much of her, you see... his mother. That dark hair and dark eyes."

"He's beautiful," I defend. I have no doubt he is, with eyes to see or not. Every part of his body is sculpted and perfect.

"You *would* think so, but you can't see him." He places the glass back to my lips and proceeds to make me drink more. I cough as it goes down having no choice but to swallow the burning liquid. "So, I hadn't thought much of him. I was hearing all these stories about a man, who was so disturbed, that instead of just burning the victims he hung them up on a hook. This is the part that started me listening, what about you?"

"You're sick!"

He places the glass back to my lips and makes me drink again. Then pulls it away again.

"Am I really? You're the one that's fucking him." He laughs, but I find no humor in his words. "He hangs them by a hook, so he can drain their blood. Doing it so it's not so messy. You know, for when he takes the saw to them."

"*Shut up!*" I scream.

"He doesn't use an electric saw. No... that would be too easy. No... instead, he uses a hand saw, just so he can hear the crunch under his hands."

A shiver runs over me. Goosebumps form on my skin.

"What's your point in all this?" My phone starts ringing in my bag, I try to move around to see if it's near but his laugh forms again as I fall over. The amount of vodka affecting me now.

"He's coming," he says.

And I know that everything *will* be fine.

CHAPTER 24

Death aka Dmitry

Anton watches me carefully. Since that phone call, I came straight to his house, no explanation at all. He takes me to where Sebastian is, tied to the chair, blood coming from his mouth and nose. He sees me and manages to smile through the swelling. I bet he knows why I'm here. I wouldn't have come any other way.

"You come to say goodbye?" Anton asks with a knife in his hand. Viktor is watching us both, then his phone pings and he looks down. Anton walks closely to Sebastian in the chair as Sebastian watches me, he doesn't care for Anton. Viktor stands, and he turns his back to us.

I pull the bar from my pants and hold it in my hand. Sebastian's eyes light up. Before Anton has the chance to turn around, I smash into the back of his head, and he drops to the floor. Viktor turns at the sound. He runs to tackle me. He's large, so when his body comes into contact with mine I drop, but don't lose the bar. As soon as we touch the ground, the bar comes up and I smack the back of his head. He doesn't stop moving, so I do it again until he does.

Sebastian's laughter fills the room as I push Viktor off of me. I don't check to make sure they're both breathing, right now I don't care. Even if they are, the ending of this isn't going to go the way I want.

"Shut up," I say finally bringing the pole down on his skull. He drops in his chair closing his eyes as I hit him. I untie and throw him over my shoulder as I walk out the house, knowing exactly where my father is.

****

Sebastian wakes up as I pull his body from the car, he falls face first onto the gravel road out the front of the house. He stands, pushing me backward and brushing the dirt from his hands and pants.

"Why did you have to knock me out as well?" he asks hands up in the air. I shrug my shoulders and turn toward the house. The door opens, and two men step out, both dressed in suits.

"Friends of yours?" I ask Sebastian, turning

back to him.

"Nope," he says coming to stand near me. We walk up the stairs, the men block it with their bodies. One puts his hands on me and pushes me back, the other nods to Sebastian. He indicates for me to lift my arms, I look to Sebastian who's staring at me like he knows what I'm about to do. He raises his eyebrows, and as the man drops to pat me down, I slide my gun out from under my jacket and fire off one single shot to his head. He drops, the other man is pulling his out when I shoot him straight through the head. I step over their bodies as I walk inside.

"He's going to be pissed," Sebastian says as we walk in. I don't care, so I don't bother answering. He isn't in the main area, so we proceed to the living room where there's no sign of them. The basement door is open, the one Sebastian used to cremate the bodies.

He points to the door saying, "Down there."

I make him go first, and as we climb down the stairs, I can hear a whimper. Then the light flickers on and I automatically spot Pollie lying on the table that slides into the burner. My father stands behind her with a drink in his hand smiling down at her.

"She's perfect, Dmitry. What she sees in you, I

don't understand."

"What did she ever see in you?" I fire back to him, referring to my mother. His nostrils flare at my comment, and he throws the glass from his hand smashing it against the wall.

"No welcome back for your Padre?" he roars with much anger in his voice.

"Why? You weren't missed by me at all," Sebastian stays, his eyes on Pollie as we speak.

"I've heard how far you've come. I came for you, did you know that?"

"I wouldn't go anywhere with you."

"You prefer them," he asks referring to Kazier.

"I prefer no one. You taught me that."

He nods his head and I watch as his hand comes down and strokes Pollie's skin. My skin, the skin on her face. His finger lifts a strand of her hair, lingering between his fingers.

"Don't touch her." I take a step forward, and he produces a knife, laying it on her bare belly. Her shirt has been pulled up, and her hands are tied down. She doesn't move, I assume she's asleep, but she isn't. Her breathing is heavy. I can see that now with the rise and fall of her breasts.

"You can choose, you know? You can have her, and work for me. But if you choose them, I *will* slice her where she lays." He digs the knife in slightly, pushing it down into her skin.

"Padre," Sebastian says, finally speaking. His eyes go to him, but he doesn't remove the knife. Before I can say or do anything, footsteps are heard echoing through from upstairs. Several of them. All our eyes focus upward.

"You brought them with you? I did warn you," he snarls.

Before he can do anything further, a knife is through his eye, just like the one Viktor delivered last time. I don't care how it happened, I rush straight over to Pollie, untying her and pulling her up to me. I hear Sebastian laugh, and when I turn around, I know why. Freya stands there with Elina next to her.

Not who I was expecting at all.

Freya walks down the stairs, pulling the knife from my father's eye then cleans it on his clothes before she pockets it back into her pants. Elina runs over and starts touching Pollie's face. Pollie pushes her hand away and starts laughing. We all look at her with wide eyes.

"Pollie, did you take anything," Elina asks concerned.

"Nope…" she hiccups laughing. I pull her closer to me thinking she's broken. Then I look up at the girls.

"How did you find us?"

Elina shrugs her shoulders like it was nothing. But it's Freya who talks.

"You're going to get your ass beat man. I saw the boys, knocked out on the floor. Wait 'til they see you." She laughs.

Elina hits her arm, and Freya snorts her nose up at her. "What, it's true… he knows it." She shrugs her shoulders.

Sebastian walks forward and takes her hand and brings it to his busted lips. She doesn't stop him, just watches.

"My padre may kill you as well if the boys don't get to you first. Shoo now," she says.

He looks back to me, with Pollie in my arms then walks away, up the stairs.

"Does Kazier know?" I ask Elina.

She touches Pollie's hair and looks up to me. "I don't have any say in how he runs anything, but I will tell him why you did what you did." I nod my head in a thank you and Freya snorts.

"Your pussy isn't gold you know." They turn to walk up the stairs, I follow them with Pollie in my arms. She's not saying much, but I know she's still awake.

"It is to him." She smirks at Freya. Freya makes choking sounds as they exit the house.

I stop just before we walk out, looking down at her. "Mine or yours?"

"Yours, but no sex."

A smile pulls at my lips as I look down at her. "No sex. Clear?"

"No hanky-panky at all. We need to talk before we venture back down that road."

I look to her and see her smiling. What's wrong with her?

"Pollie, what did he give you?"

She smirks up at me. "Vodka... the Russian drink... just like you... my Russian drink... did you know all you bitches need Jesus?" I can't help the laugh that forms after she talks non-stop. I kiss her head and place her in the car.

CHAPTER 25

Pollie

My head hurts badly, like shards of glass poking in my eyeballs and a pain of massive proportions pounds relentlessly inside my skull. I feel around me and know I'm in Dmitry's bed.

As soon as I sit my stomach starts to hurt, I scream, "Bucket."

I feel him move, my hand covers my mouth in an attempt to stop what might happen next. I feel him run and just as I bend down to throw up, a washing basket is thrust in my face and my stomach content empties all over the basket. Dmitry starts gagging as he steps away. I wipe my hand across my mouth and before I can speak I'm throwing up again. This is why I don't drink, I can't hold my liquor. I hear him gagging again, and he snatches the basket from my hands, and he does exactly what I just did, starts throwing up.

The laugh that comes feels good. This man, the one everyone is so scared of, is throwing up just on the basis of me throwing up. I laugh harder and hear him groan.

"This is not funny, Pollie."

I clutch my chest—it is, it so is. He pulls my feet pulling me to the edge of the bed, and picks me up throwing me over his shoulder, smacking my ass as he walks us to his shower. He doesn't put me down as he turns it on and climbs in with me fully clothed. Actually, when I feel the clothes, they aren't mine. He's dressed me in one of his shirts again.

The cold makes me shriek, as he slides me down his body, his very toned and naked body. He tells me to open my mouth when my feet touch the ground, then Listerine is in my mouth. I rinse and spit it out, and he does the same.

"Better?" he asks.

I nod my head. He pushes me back against the shower wall, pressing my arms up above my head, pushing his body onto me.

"Dmitry..." I breathe into him.

"Say it again," he says.

"Dmitry," I say with more oomph behind it this

time.

His hands slide up and down my body, igniting everything within me. He nips at my mouth while pulling the shirt up to my neck, then he kisses his way down until his mouth is on my breast. I push my body into him, wanting more. He doesn't hesitate and uses his hand that isn't kneading my breast and pushes down my panties. He flicks my clit, then rubs it in circles, making me move my body on his hand to create more friction.

He moves away from me, leaving me on the wall wanting more. My panties are being pulled off, and his hands are skimming my legs, rubbing over my skin. Then his mouth is on me, down there. And I can't help but moan so loudly that I scare myself with my own voice. I grab his hair, my fingers slip through its length easily. He licks, bites, nips until my legs start to shake, and my body no longer wants his mouth but his cock. I pull him by his hair, pushing his mouth away from me and upward. He lifts me, and in one instant he's in me. He doesn't move and doesn't let me move either.

"I'll try for you, Pollie, I'll try anything."

I nod my head in understanding, a tear leaving my eye.

"I know… I know," I say taking his mouth. I start

to move, he lets me. This time it's gentle, he doesn't slam into me, he doesn't tell me to bite him. He just lets me ride him the way I want. But I like what he wants, so I quicken the pace. Leaning over to his shoulder, my mouth covers a mark which I know is from my mouth, then I bite, bite hard. I feel him immediately pick up, he grabs hold of my hips, pulls me up and down, and slams me onto him. Like I'm a rag doll, and it feels like heaven. So much heaven.

"Pollie..." he says my name when he's close. I grip him harder, digging my nails into his skin. Blood coats my lips and just as he delivers the final slam of our hips meeting, my mouth detaches and I come, hard.

My body goes slack, I can't move. It doesn't bother him, to him I'm as light as a doll and easy to carry. He doesn't even struggle when he reaches down to grab a towel and wrap it around my back as he carries me back to the bed. He lays me down, kisses my lips then when he opens the door to leave, I hear him gagging again. He's removing the basket from the room, and I fall asleep with a smile on my face.

****

I wake with a hand drawing circles on my belly, I push it away and roll over trying to go back to sleep.

"I was going to steal you, and lock you up." Dmitry's voice filters through my sleepy brain. My breathing evens out, and he knows I'm awake now.

"You think that would have worked for you?" I ask him.

"Not in the slightest. But it was the only way I could think of keeping you."

"You can't force me to be with you. It has to be my decision, and mine alone."

His fingers stop, and he lies on my stomach. "Do you know what you want?"

I shake my head, because I don't. I still have no idea.

"What if I could persuade you…" His mouth latches on to my breast, and I laugh pulling him off.

"We need to talk. Seriously. But first I need to go home. I have to think."

"Why can't we talk now?"

"Okay, tell me how you feel about me?"

His body leaves mine, and he lays down next to me taking my hand in his. "Words! Why do you need them? Can't you feel it?"

"No Dmitry, I'm a woman, it doesn't work that way. Give me your words."

"I don't love you, don't go thinking that."

Shock, that's all that runs through me right at this time. My hand loosens on his, but his squeezes to keep me locked tight.

"It's so much more than that stupid word. I think you stole half of me the minute I saw you. I only feel full when you're around."

Commence wild beating heart at his words. Like crazy beating heart, it's pumping so hard in my chest.

"But you don't love me?" I ask with a small smile on my face.

He nudges me with his hand. "I don't understand that word. It was a throw around word that was used, then abused in my life. So no, I don't love you, because I never intend to use and abuse you."

I pull my hand free and stand. He doesn't move, I don't hear the bed sheets rustle at all.

"I need a standing kiss before I go," I tell him. I need him to seal his words with those lips.

Within milliseconds his hand is touching my hip

and his mouth hovers over me.

"Whether you say the word or not, cleaning up and barfing for me is love." I chuckle just as his mouth comes over mine to shut me up. He deepens the kiss and with his hands he pulls every fiber of me into him. Strangling me and I strangle him back, wanting his last breath just as he is taking mine. He finishes and his forehead is leaning gently on mine.

"When are you moving in?" he asks, his lips a minuscule distance from mine. I chuckle, even though I know what he's saying is truth. He wants that to happen more than anything.

"I still need time, Dmitry. Great sex and a confession won't change that. I need to see if I can deal with... well, you."

He pulls back slightly. "How long?"

Now standing in front of him, I shrug my shoulders. "I don't know."

"I can't take that as an answer, Pollie. I'm a creature of rhythm. I need what I do, and have to run with it just the way I like."

"Well, you changed mine the minute you carried me from the club. I guess we're even then." I reach around and drop to the floor, trying to feel for my clothes. He stops me with his hands on my shoulders and presses my clothes into my chest. They smell of vodka and my face instantly grimaces at the odor.

"You don't have to go."

"I do. I need... just me for a bit."

He walks away, leaving me there by myself. I get dressed and exit his house without a goodbye.

CHAPTER 26

Death aka Dmitry

I watch as she leaves from the couch, a taxi is already waiting out front for her. I sit in the same spot, not moving. Wondering how I can get her back without being classed as a stalker or kidnapper. Just as she pulls away, another car pulls up. I watch out the window as Anton, Viktor, and Kazier step from the car. I don't bother moving, I don't even care to open the door. They all walk with meaning in their step as they climb the stairs.

Kazier opens the door, he's the first to enter. Walking in, he spots me straight away. Anton and Viktor are next. Anton cracks his knuckles, and his chin is raised high at me. Viktor glares, his lips in a curl. They stay positioned just behind Kazier, waiting for him to speak, waiting for his orders. He walks in and takes the seat opposite me. His head drops then he lifts it back up, his eyes hard.

"You know what you did," he says. I don't give

him an answer. He sighs when nothing leaves my mouth. "Elina told me why. She even bargained with me to spare you."

Anton laughs from behind him. As soon as I look up at him, Anton shuts up, and his eyes become hard again.

"It wasn't an order from me, Death. I did *not* give you permission."

"You cracked my fucking head, you dick head," Anton chimes in his hand lifting to the back of his skull.

"You're alive," is all I give him. I didn't kill them. That will count for something.

"You put the woman in danger," Viktor says finally speaking.

I shake my head at the thought of those two idiots. "They put themselves in danger," I retort back to him.

He shakes his head at me. "There's no easy way to say this," Kazier states standing, he takes a step back, and Anton and Viktor step forward. Both their hands clenched and ready for a fight. I stand knowing what's about to happen, Viktor walks behind me, Anton stops in front of me with a smile on his face.

"This may hurt," he says.

Then I watch in slow motion as his fist comes up and connects with my face. I stumble backward into another blow which is delivered into the back of my ribs. I stand tall, Anton laughs in my face, then his fists start on my body, bruising and punishing it until I start to bend over. Viktor kicks my legs out from under me, dropping me to the floor, then kicks me in the ribs repeatedly.

Kazier's voice breaks through. "Enough."

"He knocked us out," Anton complains.

I don't hear what's said next. I don't see it either. Next thing I know, everything goes black.

****

I wake to an aching body, the sky dark. I groan and turn to my back feeling the sharp pains and bruising already crippling my body. I try to sit up and think better of it. I may lay here just a bit longer because they sure as shit made me tender as fuck. I was surprised they didn't kill me. Elina's talk must have worked.

"You look like shit." I turn my head to Anton sitting on my sofa with a bowl of ice cream in his lap. He takes a scoop and licks the spoon clean as he watches me. I sit up even through the agony trying not to wince and failing miserably. He laughs at me.

"Why are you still fucking here?" I grumble.

He shrugs his shoulders and turns the volume up on the television.

"Seriously... leave."

His eyes move from the television then down to me. "Needed to make sure you were still breathing," he scoffs taking another spoon of ice cream and then laughs at the television.

"I'm breathing... leave now!"

"Have you seen this shit? Women go crazy over it. Seriously, Magic Mike my ass. Try some magic Anton bitches."

My head drops down—is he actually watching this shit? Then the music comes on, and I know for sure that he's seriously watching crap. He scoffs at the television again.

"God, I'd lift that little bitch over my head. Where is the muscle, in his ass?"

"Anton..."

"Oh, come on, all he's doing is rubbing his cock in your face. I got some co—"

"Anton!" I yell louder, he looks down at me with his eyebrows raised.

"Go home."

"Can't, the sister is home. She drives me up the fucking wall. Kazier is fucking Elina, and Viktor is trying to not fall in love with Freya. You're my best bet tonight. Now go back to sleep." He waves his hand across effectively dismissing me. I stand and walk away from him, not being able to deal with his raggedy ass tonight.

As soon as I step into my room, her smell assaults my senses. Everywhere. She's everywhere. I groan and lay on my bed moving straight to the pillow she sleeps on. Just as I get comfortable, Anton flings my door open.

"Boss called. That man has the Doe." He nods his head out the door.

I close my eyes and think about reaching for the gun next to my bed, maybe if I shot him in his neck he wouldn't die but pass out. Nope, he would die. Fuck.

I make it slowly to the front of the house. Anton is in his car and honking the horn for me to get in—he's such an annoying prick. As soon as I climb in, he starts driving before I've even closed the damn door. I have to close my eyes at the break-neck speed he takes. Every bump in the road, we bounce high, every pot hole, we drop. And he doesn't care—At. Fucking. All. He actually blasts the music through his car, taps his hands on the wheel and sings very badly. Finally, we come to a stop at the same house we were at last time, where Viktor placed a knife through the man's eye.

CHAPTER 27

Pollie

I wake in a sweat, then I hear it, the knocking. Hearing my name called, I know it's him, I know he's back. I didn't think he'd give me much time or space, I just suspected it would be for at least one night. The knocking continues uninterrupted and constant. I walk out the cold floor beneath my feet. My hand goes to the door, his voice comes through, vibrating through my hand. I don't say a word as he speaks my name again.

"Pollie, I need... to touch you."

This wasn't the plan. I live by my plans. I needed some consistency back in my life, it went out the window the minute I met him.

"Time Dmitry," I whisper knowing he'll hear me.

"I can't do that. I just can't." He sounds so

broken.

I open the door, and he almost falls on top of me. I reach out to touch him to stop him falling, and he hisses when I come into contact with his side.

"What happened?"

His hand reaches out and runs down my face, skimming it with his fingers. "I saved you, so it's my punishment."

Shock races through me. "What do you mean?" I grab his hand and pull him inside, he shuts the door with a quiet click as he follows me in.

"I knocked out Anton and Viktor. I had to be punished. It's part of who we are."

"Why?" I don't understand what he's talking about.

"They had Sebastian, and I needed him to get to you."

I nod my head, then my heart starts beating wildly, I've been so thoughtless, so stupid. He puts me first, and he doesn't even realize he's doing it.

"Tell me about your work?"

He doesn't say much, so I rest my hand on his, squeezing it.

"If any of this is work, I need to understand. Right now, I don't understand it."

"You won't want me when I tell you." That voice is so much weaker. Not his strong, usually confident voice. It breaks me more.

"Don't you think I should decide that?"

"I relish in what I do, it's what I know. All that's ever been a constant in my life. I can't… won't… give it up, Pollie."

"I'm not asking you, too. I just need to know."

"What did he tell you? Sebastian… my father?"

My head drops and a shiver breaks through over my body. "I don't want their memories, I want the ones you can, and will, give me."

I hear him huff a breath. "How did I ever find you?" he whispers.

"You didn't, I found you," I whisper back.

"When I have bodies… vessels… I relish in it. I absolutely crave it, Pollie. It's my escape. It's like my own beautiful dark art."

"Do you drain them?" I ask, remembering the hooks. The words are stuck in the back of my mind—very disturbing images still reside there.

"Yes. Every cut I make on them has to be perfect. I can't have blood messing it up. So draining is what I have to do to make sure they are perfect."

"Keep going…"

"I work in red. It's fitting really, the red. It's significant in a way in that with each cut all the blood should be pouring out, but it isn't. So red helps me relax. Then I start the cutting, the music takes over, and my hands have a mind of their own. Each cut is clean, perfect, and precise in its delivery. Straight down to the bone."

"How long have you been doing this for?"

His hand clenches mine. "Too long. Sebastian introduced me. He was what I am to the family, but he preferred to burn them. I thought it was careless, it leaves ashes behind. What I do… it leaves nothing."

"Acid." I cringe, an internal shiver taking over my body.

"Why did you come here? Why did you warn me to not open the door when you come at night?"

"I miss the blood. You have it."

My hand pulls from his. That didn't sound

good. Actually, that's the one thing out of all his words that has scared me the most.

"Blood play?" It leaves my lips quickly. Sebastian's words are now playing over in my mind.

"Yes, I wanted to do it to you."

"That's why you left?" He doesn't speak. "You can control yourself around me, Dmitry. Why?"

He laughs dryly. "I don't know. I don't even think I want to know."

"I want you to take me there."

"Where?"

"To your room. It's in your basement, isn't it?" I can feel his stare hitting me hard.

"I don't want you down there."

That kind of hurts. I get up and walk away, he doesn't move. When I come back my violin is in my hands. I sit down and feel his stare penetrating me.

"Don't cut my throat," I joke with him, but he doesn't respond. I feel him tense near me. "Violin... the name comes from a Medieval Latin word *Vitula,* it means stringed instrument..." when he doesn't speak I stroke the G-string, "...the hairs on mine are horse hair." I place the bow to all the strings. "When the violin was invented, did you know it was made of sheep gut?" I press the bow to the strings playing a cord, then stopping. "Niccolo Paganini is the best violinist to ever live. They say he sold his soul to the devil to be able to play so well." I start to play Stubborn Love by the *Lumineers.*

He doesn't move as I play, I didn't expect him to, and soon I forget he's even there. Soon the melody takes over, and the only thing that draws me from it is his hand touching my leg. It pulls me from the music, and I set the bow down, breathing heavily.

"You just came into my world, I want to go to yours."

"Mine isn't as beautiful as yours."

I press my hand to his face. "It is, you're beautiful."

His lips press to mine, just a soft kiss. I feel him nod his head on mine. "Sleep now," he says standing and picking me up under my legs. He carries me to my room, placing me on the bed and climbing in next to me. I turn, and he pulls me into him, wrapping me in his arms and holding my hand tightly.

As if I would ever let it go.

CHAPTER 28

Death aka Dmitry

Her sleeping form is so innocent, each time she moves in her sleep, it pains me. The bruises covering my body have only grown more sensitive. She lies near me, her hand still in mine, her ass stuck to my cock. I couldn't even give her the time she wanted away from me. How will I be able to survive without her once she enters that room and realizes how fucked I am, and how perfect she is. Maybe I can lie to her. Take her somewhere else in the house, tell her that's where I work, but I don't want to lie to her. I don't want to lie to her about anything.

She rolls over, and when she does her elbow hits my ribs. I groan, and she sits up. Her hands pull up my shirt, and her soft fingers skim my chest. She runs over it slowly, gently touching the bruising that's formed. Then she goes to my face, her thumb pads over my bottom lip.

"Thank you for protecting me," she whispers kissing my bottom lip then standing. She walks out and I hear her open and close the fridge. She comes back with an ice pack in her hand and places it on my smarting ribs. Holding it down with one hand as she lays back down. "I don't have to work this weekend," she says her leg coming up between mine.

"So you're mine all weekend?" I ask, and she nods her head, her long eyelashes fan across her cheek.

"So, take me to yours," she says standing. I sit up and watch her as she pulls up a pair of jeans over her ass. Then she throws the shirt that she sleeps in to the ground, pulling on another, with no bra.

Off to mine we go, I guess.

****

When the door closes behind us, she tucks her hands into the back of her pants. She stands there and waits for me to take her where she wants to go. I grab her hand, and walk to the door, pressing my hand to the reading device for it to open, then we walk down the stairs.

One body remains. I haven't had the chance to dispose of it yet. Her hand lingers on the wall as we reach the bottom.

"The smell," she says, not questioning just pointing it out.

"I have exhaust fans," I say, then flick them on. The exhaust fans have been fitted with special devices to remove the offensive smell before they expel the putrid odor into the air above my house.

"Is there anywhere I can sit?" she asks not moving.

I grab her hand and take her to my stool, pushing it away from the body and over near the stairs where she stands for her to sit on.

"Okay, do what you do. Don't mind me."

I almost want to laugh at that. I refrain and step back from her trying not to think about her being here as I start my routine. I turn the music on which is usually programmed to activate anyway, but this time I pre-empted and flicked the switch to off upon entering. The heavy metal blasts through the basement and she covers her ears at first, then slowly removes them. I always forget her other senses are more heightened. Then I pull the body from the hook, carrying it to the table. When I drop it on, she looks up, she heard the sound. I pick up the saw, looking at her. She doesn't look afraid, she just sits there trying to hear everything I'm doing. I can only imagine what she's thinking—crazed.

I glance away, I can't look at her when I start to cut. The saw slices beautifully through the skin, the first bone crunches under the edge of the saw, then deeper, and deeper, until sweat starts to form on my forehead. My ribs hurt, the pressure I need to use to cut through is extracted from all of my body. And when you saw, you feel every inch of it.

Then the adrenaline takes over, and numbs the pain. Before I know it, I have two arms removed. I only stop briefly because a hand touches my hip.

I turn to see Pollie there, she leans up and whispers in my ear, "Keep going." I look back to the body, then to her. She's now facing downward, her hands are on my pants. She undoes the first button, then pulls the zipper down and gets to her knees. Pulling my pants down as she does. Her hand wraps around my cock. She strokes it softly, then her mouth covers it, and she licks the tip, massaging my balls with her free hand. Then in one swift movement, almost all of me is in her mouth and down her throat. My hands clench the saw tight, it presses downward straight through the bones. With each thrust the saw moves as well. Each lick of her tongue, my hips and saw buck. I close my eyes as she swirls her tongue around. Letting go of the saw, and pulling her upward, she kicks her pants off, dropping them to the ground. I lift her and place her ass on the table.

"Don't move backward, don't shift your hands," I tell her, because if she does, all she will feel will be the coldness of the body, which is only inches from her bare ass. She moans as I pull her closer, my cock at the tip of her pussy. I pull her forward, her hands go backward to hold herself up, but I stop them just in time and pull them back to me.

Then I slam into her, her head flies back, and she moans loudly in my ear. Screaming my name.

"Tell me about it," she moans in my ear. "Tell me about your blood play," she says.

I continue to push into her, wondering if I ever really liked it. Because with her, I don't need it, all I need is her. "Just as my cock enters you…" I emphasize with a slam, and she screams, "…I cut you…" my finger runs along her back pretending to slice with my finger, "…not deep enough to need stitches, just enough so I can lick it."

She shivers and I know she's close. I'm right there with her.

"Do you want to cut me?" she asks leaning over and biting my shoulder, her teeth digging in and puncturing the skin. She licks it, then kisses me, giving me a taste myself on her.

"Never. This skin..." I say slapping her ass, "...is never to be marked. It's too perfect. If anyone mars your flawless skin, I'll cut the skin from their bones."

She collapses into me when she finally comes. I fuck her harder, then she lays her head on my shoulder, breathing me in.

"Well shit! Who needs to buy porn when you two are here?" Anton's voice booms from the top of the stairs, he's looking down at us smiling. I pull Pollie's shirt down, covering her ass and grab the closest thing I can and throw it at him. He ducks the saw that was aimed at his head and turns and walks back up the stairs.

"Did he just see us?" I brush her hair from her face. "With the body..." Her head turns to where the body is, but she doesn't say anything else.

"No, he just came down," I say easing her when really I have no idea when he arrived. She relaxes and I pull her from the table, grabbing her jeans and dressing her. She smirks at me when I do it. Her lashes fluttering over her eyes. I grab her hand once we are both dressed and pull her up the stairs.

When we reach the top it's not just Anton, it's all of them. In my fucking house. Like it's some episode of Friends. Fucking hell. Whatever happened to leaving me alone? Freya and Viktor are close together as they stand near the door. Anton stands near Kazier and Elina, who are smirking at us.

"They're all smiling at us aren't they?" Pollie whispers to me. I don't tell her only some are, I just tell her no.

"Why the fuck are you all here?"

Kazier steps forward. "The Italian scums have declared war," Kazier says.

Elina scoffs at him. "I'm Italian, you asshole." She hits him in the chest, and he winces.

"Yeah, but you have a Russian in you all the time," he jokes with her. She immediately follows that with a kiss.

"Pollie won't be safe. No one will be safe. I've come into possession of a house, it's large. Get your shit, you're both coming with us."

My eyes go wide, I'm sure of it. Then my head shakes, not happening. "Get out."

"Do you want to protect her? Numbers are

safer," Elina says.

"You think I want to live with you? I don't want to live with anyone… ever. I don't do people… ever. I stand you because I have to. I prefer the dead. So if anyone comes to mine that are unwelcome, there's only one way they will end up… on my preferred list, dead."

Pollie steps away from me, withdrawing. Then I realized what I've just said.

"Leave," I tell them, facing her hurt face. "Now…" I bark louder not even looking at them.

"Pollie…" She looks down, not answering me. "Pollie…" I say again.

I hear the front door close.

"You don't want me?"

I drop my head. "I think you're the only thing I do need in this life. I didn't need anything but my bodies before you, Pollie."

She nods her head but doesn't say a word.

CHAPTER 29

Pollie

"We have to go there today," I tell him, we spent the night at his house. Anton came back later that day. I think he really likes Dmitry, but he also likes to fuck with him. I can hear the playfulness in his voice. He respects him, and Dmitry just doesn't realize it yet.

"Where?" he asks walking up behind me. His hands clasp onto my stomach, his head leans into the nook of my neck. Kisses trail up my neck as I wash my hands.

"The house. You can't ignore them."

He grumbles against my neck. "Why can't I just stay locked up with you?"

I don't dwell too much about what he said last night. He was angry. Plus, he made it up to me—all of last night. My senses, my emotions, all are heightened when he touches me. When he takes me as his.

"They're your family. Let's go," I say pulling away from his touch. His hand grabs hold of mine.

"I don't need them, though, all I need and want is you. And I will have you, Pollie."

Laughter bursts from me. "All macho man," I tease him.

He pulls my hips into his, I can feel he's ready to go.

I place a kiss on his chin. "Go, now."

He hisses at me, and I laugh as I pull away and walk to the front door, knowing he will follow me. Just as I pull the door open, I run straight into someone, a woman. Her hands go to my shoulders, holding me upright. I immediately start apologizing, and she laughs at me.

"Sweetheart, no sweat." Her nails dig into my skin before she removes them. "What beautiful skin you have." I can feel that she's closer now, assessing me. I take a step back, waiting for Dmitry to walk out.

"Thank you," is all I can think to say.

"I'm Amy, and what's your name?"

"Pollie." Her hand comes up and holds my hand lifting it up. She rubs the surface of it, and when I try to pull it away, she holds harder not letting me go.

"Drop her hand, Amy." Dmitry's voice blares from behind me. She does as he says, her nails scraping along my hand. I feel as she pushes past me, brushing me to the side.

"Sebastian told me where you live now." I can hear her heels clicking on the floor as she walks around me. "It's been too long, lover. Too long. No need for me now that you have a doll?"

I know she's looking at me. I hear the sound of a zipper opening. My mouth drops, I hope I'm hearing things.

"Pull your shirt back up."

"You know I can play with more than just you. She can join in. I would love to play with her skin. Tell me, have you marked it yet?"

He doesn't respond, and her heels click closer to me. They come to stop when she's in front of me. She grabs my hand, lifts it, and places it on her skin. When I realize it's her breast, I try to pull away, but she won't let me.

"Can you feel the scars? That's all him. Do you

have them?" She runs my hand up and down her breasts, her voice changes direction as she speaks to Dmitry. "Think of the possibilities, don't you want it?"

"Dmitry..." I say, pulling my hand away harder. Tugging at it.

"I miss it," I hear the small voice coming from him.

I drop my head and feel with my left hand for the door handle. When I find it open, I walk out. Not stopping as I almost break into a jog, listening to the traffic surrounding me. When I feel I am far enough away, I stop. Pull my phone from my ear and call Elina.

****

"Pull over," I scream. Elina pulls the car over, and I manage to push the door open just in time for my stomach to empty itself.

"Are you sick?" she asks me.

I shake my head. I haven't been.

"Are you pregnant?" She laughs as I shut the door and she drives off.

My eyes go wide.

How long ago was my last period?

Shit. Fuck. I cover my mouth.

"Fuck, I was kidding." She pulls the car hard to the right, my head bangs on the window.

"Elina," I say rubbing my head. "What's gotten into you?"

She stops the car, and I hear the car door slam. I wait, unsure of what's happening. Then as soon as she's back, she throws a box at me.

"My house or yours?" she says starting the car.

"What is it?"

"Pregnancy test."

"I can't be. I don't want to be. I mean… gosh… I don't even know."

"We don't know anything yet. Just wait, I'm pulling into yours now."

She stops the car, and I take a shaky step down. Every emotion running through me.

What will I do if I am?

Would he want a child?

What happens if he hates me?

Then I remember the anger from before and don't care what he wants because it's more about me than him.

After moving inside, Elina says, "Pee on this." She places a stick into my hand, and I nod my head and walk to the bathroom, almost in a daze. When I sit on the toilet, nothing happens, then the door opens and a tap starts running. "Water helps," Elina says not moving.

I drop my head into my hands and try to not think of why I'm sitting on a toilet trying to pee with a woman watching and waiting for me. "Pee already. Before he tracks me here, and busts open your door," she says referring to Kazier.

I laugh and start to pee placing the stick between my legs then holding it out once I'm done. Elina takes it from my hands while I finish up.

"Two minutes," she chimes just as her phone starts ringing. "Yeah, yeah, she's with me." I wait for her finish. "It's Kazier, Death went to his looking for you."

"You didn't tell him where we are, did you?"

"No, but what happened? You were working things out yesterday, weren't you?"

I shrug my shoulders. "We were until *she* showed up."

"It's positive, Pollie."

"Fuck!" I swear leaving the bathroom. "Fuck, fuck, *fuck!*" I say again.

Elina laughs behind me. "You're swearing... out loud. I take it you aren't happy?"

"I need to see a doctor."

"Yes, you do. We need to see how far along you are." Banging starts on my front door. "Shit!" she says walking away and leaving me to sit on the bed. My head's hurting, too much information now running rampant in my head.

"Where is she?" I hear his voice come through the walls then his footsteps as he walks to where I am.

I lay down on the bed and don't move. Right now, I couldn't care less what he says.

"Pollie, I told you last time not to leave me like that." I don't answer him, and stay where I am, lying on the bed. My hands cling to the sheets, my head is almost hanging over the side the bed. "Pollie..." he speaks his voice getting closer. "Pollie... answer me?"

I don't, there's no need to. I hear Elina, she doesn't say a word as she walks in and sits beside me.

"What did you do now?" she asks him. He snarls at her and storms off. I hear the bathroom door shut, and that makes me jump up. I run straight to it and smack into his chest.

"Elina, leave," he says while my hands grip onto his chest. I can feel his breathing, and it's becoming harder and harder, I can hear it being forced through his nostrils. I remove my hands and take a step back.

"Pollie, do you want me to leave?" Elina asks ignoring Dmitry's anger in his voice.

"It's fine," I say to him, to her, but more to myself. I listen as she walks out. Her heels tapping on the floor and then the front door shuts.

CHAPTER 30

Death aka Dmitry

She backs away slowly, her hands to her sides. My eyes go back to the stick in my hand. I may not be up with everyday normal, but this stick, I know exactly what it is.

"How was your *friend*?" she snaps walking away from me. "Didn't stay to play?"

I love the sound of venom in her voice—jealousy at its best. "You left. *Again*. Even after we had this talk last time."

Her spine stiffens at my comment, she walks to the sound of my voice and throws a punch to my chest. "You wanted her." Another punch.

"No, I didn't. I said I missed it. If you would've stayed a second longer, you would've known that."

"If I can't fulfill you then it's not going to work."

I grip her arm, holding it tightly. "Tell me what

you want? Tell me, Pollie?" I can hear the anguish in my voice as I ask her.

She looks down to the floor. Not speaking for a few seconds then she says, "I just want you. I want you to want me to be enough."

"You are enough," I tell her because she is.

"I don't associate with death, Dmitry. I associate with life."

My hands grip her face. "Don't you see... you are what brings life into me? Do you even realize it? Every time you breathe near me, it fills my soul, sparking life back into me. Only you can do that."

"I'm pregnant, and it's yours."

I cock my head at that. "I sure as shit hope to fucking God it's mine, woman."

Her lips twitch up at me. "Do you even want kids?" she asks me.

The answer to that is simple, no. Hell to the fuck, no. I don't want to bring in any kids into this life of mine, not a hope in a hell. This life is nothing but torture, depression, darkness. Apart from Pollie, that is. I look up to her, she bites her lip as she waits for my answer. So innocent, so sweet. She has no idea. A child that would come from her, I have no doubt would be fine with the amount of *'love'* she would give. Even if that word doesn't mean shit to me, it does to her.

"No," I answer her truthfully. Her face drops, her lip red now from biting it. "Dark, Pollie, dark is all I am. You want a kid around that?"

Her head starts shaking no.

"You cut me, do you remember that? Any sane woman wouldn't have stepped within feet of you after that. But I could feel something you kept hidden from everyone else. Something that was only there when I was around. So yes, I want to have kids with you. This kid in particular." Her hand touches her belly. "So now it's your turn. Give me the chance that I have given you. It will work because we work. Anything that comes from us will work.''

My eyes close tightly. Why must she crawl inside me like she does?

"Pack your shit, you're moving out," I say to her.

A smile etches on her face, she knows she's won this round, so far.

I watch as she moves, walking slowly to her bag, then pauses. I can feel her uncertainty. She shouldn't have any, none at all. I would give her my last breath if I could. "Don't hesitate, stop thinking, Pollie." She nods her head and starts to pack her bag throwing as many clothes into it as possible, then she's offering me her hand. I take it, knowing I'm keeping her for life.

****

"I think we should try it," Pollie says lying next to me. The doctor just left and checked for a fetal heartbeat. I heard the fetal heartbeat of *my* child. That still amazes me. And makes me want to cut my own throat from these feelings I have, for something that I don't understand.

"Try what?" I ask her. She brushes her fingers over her stomach being in as much shock as me, her eyes starting to tear. It was the last thing both of us expected. Especially me. No one brings children around me, it's the truth. Yet, here we are, wanting to bring one into the world, and calling it our own.

"Blood play," she answers. Her fingers stop moving on her belly, and I begin to shake my head.

"Not in this fucking life, your skin is to not be harmed."

"Seriously, what are you going to think when this baby pushes my skin out? I'll get stretch marks, marring this skin. What happens if I cut myself, and leave a scar? Will you still want me then?"

It doesn't take me long to answer. "Yes, of course, but it will never happen under my hands."

"Why can't I cut you?"

I think about that for a second. Then reach over and pull a knife from the drawer. I sit up on the bed, removing my clothes, then my hands touch her hips and pull her pants off along with her panties and then her top. She moves with me, no words needed as I undress her. I take her waist lifting her from the bed and placing her on my lap. She wiggles and I slap her ass to keep her still.

"Hand." She raises her hand—palm upward—I place the knife into it, and her palm closes around it. "Steady," I tell her bringing it down, just to the right of my chest. Her hand begins to shake and I pause, she steadies herself taking a deep breath. "Just enough to draw blood." She nods her head, and the coolness of the knife's blade touches my skin. "Slice, Pollie."

Her head shakes, no. But her hands move. Her first cut is so small that only a droplet of blood squeezes out. I ask her to do it again, but she shakes her head.

"I don't like it. I don't want to hurt you like that."

"You bite me, Pollie, drawing blood. Don't deny you don't like it. I feel the way your body reacts to it." She starts to scoot downward, her hands coming between us. She inserts my cock into her, her head going back when I'm fully inside her.

"I'll bite you, Death." Her voice is sexual. Turned on. She starts to move, riding back and forth, back and forth. Her arms go behind her, holding my thighs. Her hair dangles freely, touching my legs. Her breasts so full, bounce every move she moves. She may be the calm to my storm, but she brings the lightning without even realizing it.

I sit up, wrapping my arms around her, she lets me. Her head staying back, I pull her hair to my neck, she leans forward and bites down hard. Then again, and again. Rocking, and bobbing into me. Like I'm her last meal. I could fuck her every day, and never get sick of it, or sick of her. She is like nothing else. And it's pure joy to have her.

****

"Dmitry," Pollie's voice calls down to me.

I'm draining a body. She knows and won't step a foot through the door. I rinse my hands and walk up the stairs. As soon as I reach the doorway, my feet move fast, my heart hammers in my chest. "Dmitry…" Her voice sounds again, she won't stop me. My hands are around his throat, his head slams back into the wall, his eyes go wide.

"Let him speak, Dmitry." Her voice now closer. Smoother. Calming. I take a deep breath, and my grip loosens but doesn't dissolve.

"Why are you here? Do you want to be downstairs?" I ask him. His hand taps my hand, telling me to loosen. I do but only minutely, just enough for him to speak.

"I came to apologize, I'm going back to Russia. I have to clean up *his* mess."

"Apologize?" I scoff at him.

"His hands wouldn't have ever been on her if you hadn't said anything."

Sebastian's eyes look over to Pollie, and I squeeze tighter. His eyes leave her. "Have you told her how you feel, Dmitry? Don't be like him. Tell her."

My hand drops from his throat, I point to the door. "Out, or you won't ever leave here again."

He nods and looks back to me one last time

before he walks out closing the door behind him. I turn to Pollie who's just standing there.

"Do I need to tell you?" I ask as she steps closer toward the sound of my voice.

"I'm a woman, Dmitry. We always need the words."

I shake my head at her. Place her hand on my heart. "It beats just for you. If you die, I'll follow. You know that, right?"

She nods her head. "You die, I die. Got it?" She smirks at me.

"I would hunt you if someone took you. I would find you, and I would destroy anybody in my way."

"Got it!" She laughs this time.

"You want that fucking word, don't you?" I roll my eyes at her.

"Just once. Say it just once for me," she begs. She has asked me several times over the last few days for *that word* to be uttered from my mouth.

"Does it really mean that much to you?"

"Yes. And I want to record it, so I can play it back every time I think you're being and ass, and threating to kill everyone for me." Her hands start feeling around the table for her phone, she presses a few buttons and holds the phone up to my mouth. "Tell me, handsome, tell me."

"I, Dmitry Smirnov... love you, Pollie... soon to be Smirnov."

She drops the phone to the floor. Her mouth open wide. "Is that? Is that?" She can't finish her question. I grab her hand and slide a ring onto her finger, tears leaving her eyes and traveling down her cheeks. "Hold up. You only putting a ring on it because I'm knocked up?"

"No. The ring is so I can keep you... and fuck you... anytime I want."

"Well, that's a given." She laughs pushing her hips into mine, and she places a kiss up to my lips with a smile on her face. "One more time..." her mouth moves against mine, "...say it, one more time."

"Love you, Pollie."

She squeals and jumps into my arms, wrapping her legs around me.

I know I'm going to get laid tonight, now that's a given.

CHAPTER 31

Dmitry aka Death

Pollie's belly is bigger now. She's just moved from her first trimester, which is meant to be the scariest. Her tits are my dream land—so plump, so sensitive.

She walks out with nothing on, throwing her dress to the ground. Oh, and she's also extremely moody, which I secretly love.

"Nothing fits me!"

I don't say a word, last time I did, I had a shoe thrown at my head. Her hands go up in the air before she walks back into the closet. I sit and wait on the bed for her, this time when she emerges she has on a dress that clings to her body. Her belly pokes out, and her tits are on full display.

"Don't you dare say a word, this is all that fits."

"I wasn't going to," I say standing and moving to her. Things have been better. She made a deal with me—I had to build a door to the basement coming in from outside of the house. She didn't want the bodies brought in through our front doorway anymore. I agreed, and now she's asked me to only work when she sleeps. Which I've also agreed to, especially since she sleeps so much.

She doesn't want me down there when she's here. Pollie wants me to choose life over death. I've been trying. The itch to cut and get lost in it all is becoming easier. Especially now that she is here. She knows when I want to get lost—she removes her clothes and places her hands on her body. At Kazier's wedding, which was only a few weeks ago—happening in complete secret this time, so no one was shot—I couldn't handle the happiness. The fullness of it invading me. She pulled me to the bathroom as my fists tightened, backed me into the wall, then slid her shirt off placing my hands on her skin. It's an instant relaxation. *She is it.* Those moments when the only time I could calm down was to lose myself in the basement have lessened, and now all I want to do is lose myself in her. Belly and all.

"Am I fat? Tell me now?" Her hands go to her hips.

I stand and remove them, kissing her breasts,

her very high and exposed breasts.

"No, you're stunning."

She smirks up at me. "You just want sex tonight. You don't have to sweet talk me for that, you know that's a given." She smiles as she walks off. Every night, sometimes twice a day, she crawls onto my lap pulling my cock free. I hope it's not just the hormones, I hope it stays like that even after the pregnancy. Otherwise, she will stay pregnant the rest of her life.

"We're going to be late," I tell her.

She walks in carrying a pair of shoes, a bag in her hand. "Come on then." She waves her hands around.

Tonight Kazier's father is throwing a party. He does this often to keep up reputation. He's in politics now. Lord knows who voted that man in. He would slice all their throats while reading them a bedtime story.

****

"It sounds busy," Pollie says with her hand through mine as we walk the stairs of the mansion. A doorman greets us with a glass of champagne. I take it sipping as we enter. I find Kazier in his usual spot, no Elina. She isn't allowed to come to these gatherings. She is, after all, the family's enemy. And every time he has to come, he looks about ready to kill someone. Freya, Viktor, and Anton all sit near him at the table. His hands start tapping on the glass in front of him. He's now agitated.

"Holy shit, Polls. Look at that belly… and tits," Anton says.

I throw my glass straight at his head, he dodges and shrugs his shoulders.

"You told me I wasn't fat?" she hisses leaning up to me.

I lean down to her. "You aren't."

"Oh yeah… you fat. You got a fat ass, all right."

Pollie's mouth drops open at Anton's comment, and Freya smacks him hard across the back of the head.

"You look beautiful, Pollie, Anton's just jealous is all."

I pull the nearest seat out for her to sit on. She kicks her heels off under the table as soon as she sits. Kazier continues to tap the glass, not even acknowledging his father when he walks in and addresses him.

"Kazier…" he says louder. I bang my knee to his

since I'm the closest, and he looks up at his father with cold eyes.

"Have you told him yet?"

His eyes move away from his father's, then he looks over to Viktor. He raises his glass in the air. "You're marrying Freya next week. Congratulations."

Viktor's mouth drops open, he looks at Kazier, gauging to see if it's the truth. When not another word leaves his mouth, he stands throwing the seat back as he does. Freya sits in her spot, not moving, her eyes on her hands.

"This is a joke, right?" Viktor looks around to all of us ascertaining our reactions.

Anton is actually quiet for the first time.

"You all knew, didn't you?" he accuses. His fists clench, then unclench. His nostrils flare.

"You fuck," Freya screams, throwing a plate from the table at him. It misses his head, and before she can say anything else, she runs from the room.

"You can't choose who I marry," Viktor says to Kazier and his father, anger still etched all over his face.

"We can, and we did!" Kazier's father speaks.

Viktor ignores him and looks down to Kazier, who hasn't spoken.

"Look at me," Viktor snaps. Kazier's eyes look up to meet Viktor's. "You can't make me marry her."

Kazier slams his glass onto the table, smashing it with his hands. I can see the blood that forms around his fingertips. As it drips down, he sits there watching it, clenching his hands to bring more blood to the surface. He stands, his hand landing on the table, blood smearing as he does. Pollie squeezes my leg under the table, and I squeeze hers back.

"Don't for one second deny you have feelings for her. She is still to be married. Would you have preferred I marry her to Anton? Death perhaps?"

Pollie's nails dig in deeper. I haven't told anyone we're getting married. There hasn't been any need to. They'll know once it's done. I won't risk her life by telling people. I explained this to her, and she understands since she saw what happened at Elina's and Kazier's first wedding.

"Fuck off! Don't bring me into this," Anton complains. He actually looks angry. Is it for Viktor? I don't know.

"Does she not have a say in this?"

Kazier's head drops. I turn to look for his father and see he's already left, leaving his son to clean the mess like always.

"No. No, she doesn't. Her father approves, and this *is* to happen. He will not be happy if another one is canceled."

"So I'm it then?" Viktor states, glaring at him now.

"You are, and be fucking happy. I know you want to fuck her."

"*I don't want marriage... ever,*" Viktor screams.

Kazier salutes him as he walks to the door. "Too fucking bad," is all he replies before he disappears.

I grab Pollie's hand to help her stand. Clinging to me she doesn't say a word as we walk out the door. When we reach the car, she hugs me tight.

"I love you, Dmitry," she whispers into my battered soul. Pulling her half out whenever she's near, stealing it with just one breath.

I take a deep breath, feeling it, feeling her. "I too, Pollie, I too."

She giggles knowing I hate the "L" word.

"I know." She leans up, planting a kiss on my

cheek.

THE END

Book 3 –
Viktor's story, to be released 2017

If you would like to keep updated on releases, you can join my mailing list here: Newsletter

You can join my fan group here: Fan Group

Thank you so much for reading my words. I hope they seeped into you and made you feel something… good or bad.

If you would kindly leave a review from the site you purchased it from, it would be greatly appreciated.

EVERY REVIEW counts.

Good or bad.

Please.